DAVID ARSCOTT

Cultic Cyphers
from
Celtic Cyprus (7,5)

First published in 2002 by Pomegranate Press,
Dolphin House, 51 St Nicholas Lane,
Lewes, Sussex BN7 2JZ
pomegranatepress@aol.com

British Library Cataloguing-in-Publication Data.
A catalogue record for this book is available from the
British Library

ISBN 0 9542587 0 3

Printed by MFP Design & Print, Longford Trading Estate,
Manchester M32 0JT

For Jill

FOREWORD by E. Engelbert Thoite

President, Thoite Ozarks Real Estate
& Development Inc.

Because no sensible publishing house would think of touching a product like this, I was happy to volunteer myself as the necessary source of private patronage to get Douglas O'Dale's labor of love onto the shelves of the bookstores and libraries. It has not turned out to be the thing I expected, but promises are made to be kept. Whether it has a chance of fighting its corner against more regular books I do not pretend to know, words not being my business, but I can promise you there are some quaint things in it, and that the man who put it together was a fascinating and unusual kind of guy.

I knew O'Dale for only the last few weeks of his life, but it was time enough for the pair of us to get a warm friendship started up. No doubt the relationship was a mite uneven by virtue of the fact he was introduced to me as a more or less penniless Britisher who needed a retreat for some reason private to himself. I know how grateful he was to be given the run of my outdoor leisure complex during that off-season period and I tried not to make him feel obligated and humble. That was how I got myself involved in this project, making an effort to take his concerns seriously so he could still feel every bit a man.

You might be inclined to ridicule someone who did nothing much else but fuss with the alphabet, and I have to tell you I am unable to view it as a proper and useful activity for a healthy human being, but O'Dale was not the trembling pansy you might easily suppose. I liked the fellow. He had brains and humor, and I believe I might have helped make something notable of him had things panned out differently.

What can I tell you about him? He was around fifty, some good way above six feet, and weighing in at I suppose 140 pounds. He was gangly and awkward, and I can just see him tipping himself out of a rowboat while trying to fish an oar out of the water. Whatever a few big mouths have said (and there could be a nasty shock for some of them when the courts get to work on it) there is no shred of evidence to suggest anything else, and until such time as anything extra comes to light I shall remain firmly of the belief that it was a complete accident.

In the first days I admit I took him for some kind of windy intellectual, but you had to get past the prissy accent and the long words. I used to drive up to check on my property, and we would fall to talking, and I never did find anyone more interested in the affairs of the business world. He was hugely enthralled by all my real estate stories, and although I always told him to stop me when he had had enough, he never once did.

As for the crossword puzzles, I am not greatly the wiser, but he sure had me hooked for a while. When he first showed me the kind of trickery he could do with words my head was in a bit of a spin, and I even tried my hand at it myself. It is nothing but a waste of time, and it is finally beyond my comprehension, but I admit that it is fulsome smart. My disappointment is that this book is not what I thought was coming. Sure, if you read through it hard enough I think you will discover not a few hints about how to solve a puzzle, but it is too damned complicated for a beginner like me. However, perhaps I am one of a dying breed, which it would not surprise me to learn.

As you will see, O'Dale involved several of his old friends in this project, getting them to put up clues for him. I did make some tentative enquiries through contacts of mine over in England, but I was unable to trace a single one of them. Never mind. There is nothing libellous in here, and I see no good reason to hold up publication while we track them all down.

I would like, in closing, to offer grateful thanks to my secretary, Anita Bly, who has done so much to bring this thing out into the light of day. Anita has a sensitivity to words herself, and it is entirely down to her that what I am putting onto the dictating machine reads right on the page, with the slang of an uncultured man taken out of it and all the proper marks and periods put in. She even suggested the weird title of the book which, now she has explained it to me, I think mighty cunning and just right.

Douglas O'Dale's pages have not been changed at all. He had written everything out in a very clear hand, so I simply packaged it all up and sent it off to the printer with instructions to leave it as it was, even to the strange English spellings where they are different from our own accepted standard. Anita has been through everything to check it out, and the book is just how O'Dale wrote it.

So here it is. Make what you can of it. Friends assure me it is a prime candidate for the pulping machine, but this is a strange world we live in and I like to think, as the song says, that it is not necessarily so.

E. Englebert Thoite

Carthage, Missouri

CULTIC CYPHERS
FROM
CELTIC CYPRUS (7,5)

Mr Douglas O'Dale's
unique guide to solving
cryptic crossword puzzles

If, as the sapient T.S. Eliot asserted, a limerick may be as finely wrought a work of art as a Petrarchan sonnet, why be bashful about the claims of the crossword puzzle? Limericks may have a longer pedigree, but they lack the resonance which lifts the greatest clues into the realms of art. Indeed, whereas nobody can pretend that Eliot was making other than an ultimately commonplace (if deliberately provocative) point about the marriage of content and form, he would surely have conceded that the best crossword clue soars above dull cleverness: it creates life.

Even the humble anagram, all too often the wan compiler's feeble gimcrack – it, too, may work this magic trick. Do we regard it as mere coincidence that evil shamefacedly shuffles into the confession that it is vile? Or that frisky, hyperactive Eros should become uncomfortably sore? Or that T.S. Eliot himself, so painstaking and relatively unproductive a poet, should return unambiguously branded as one of literature's drudges? Granted, other words may be construed from the same letters ('litotes', in this case, being not the least appropriate), but to discover the hidden truths of the lexicon is to share the quick joy of some religious celebrant who, in a blessed state of grace, is permitted to partake of the Mystery.

The crossword clue offers a restless harmony, the startling confluence of two worlds which, by verbal necessity, become not simply superimposed but, mixing their colours, produce a new and more wonderful hue. To devise the simplest of examples: *Dog comes back to find his master (3)*. What I shall henceforth call the 'surface' clue is perhaps pleasantly domestic. We may enjoy the image of the faithful hound bounding in at the door to fling itself, slobbering, upon a beloved owner. Or (for the imagination is an infinitely resourceful beast) we may picture a more macabre scene in which a whimpering, bedraggled creature sniffs its way through the snows, following a tenuous trail of scent to where a man lies crumpled and semi-conscious beneath the detritus of an avalanche. Or perhaps . . . but I have no wish to waste paper. Choose your image. I believe the literary theorists who have followed Mr Eliot regard an apparent randomness of response as exemplary.

As for the 'subterranean' clue (another essential term), here it is disappointingly trite. The letters of *dog* are to be reversed through a painfully threadbare 'signal' (*comes back*) and *master*, we then realise, is to be interpreted as the supreme being. Perhaps we may argue that Master in the Christian usage usually refers to the Son rather than the Father, but let us show ourselves a fitting charity on this occasion.

Now we have, fleetingly, two disparate worlds, one (the surface clue) in which a faithful animal does the decent thing, another (the 'solution') which owes allegiance to a divine presence. Are we not briefly touched (even the most pressed-for-time strap-hanger on the 8.15) to bring the two into conjunction, perhaps to analogise the exuberance of shaggy, prancing Rover with the effusiveness of a charismatic convert, or the suffering victim of the snows (however supposedly masterful) with fallen mankind yet sought out by an indefatigable Redeemer? The effect is like the bright flash of light struck by the wheel of a train on its electric rail, the separate objects creating a beautiful, brilliant spark.

A more complex clue yields even richer splendours: *Does he entreat soft complaisance in the car? (6).* The solution is, of course, *prayer* (one who prays), and there is a particularly fine blue flash as notions of piety meet the images of amorous adventure suggested by the surface clue. Do we not envisage a man of the cloth betrayed by his inner demon into an outrageous assault on an innocent member of his flock? But the subterranean clue offers several appetising complications.

For the impatient or inexperienced I shall prosaically parse this clue: *p* stands for *piano*, or in this instance soft; *aye* betokens complaisance; and *RR* is the car which needs no name. Only a linguistic dullard could ignore the many fertile associations here, among them music, political debate, luxury, gleaming efficiency. What a flavoursome pot-pourri!

My first purpose in jotting down a few thoughts on the subject was simply to make a case for the best possible puzzles, while throwing in a few necessary directions for those new to the art. Surface clues, I was going to insist – and still do – should be coherent in themselves and should create distinctive mental scenes, whether humorous, horrific or plain homely. Tear the grid from the page and these few lines should yet be the most suggestive in any newspaper. Subterranean clues should be unimpeachably fair and should display and demand a play of wit. The solutions should be pleasing in themselves: words which nourish or excite.

Yet the more I advanced with my project the more I felt drawn to reveal the profundity of experience which might be encapsulated by our hermetic square. I had solicited such of my former friends and acquaintances as might be supposed willing to help furnish suitable clues for the puzzle I had created, and their response was, to say the least, disquieting. Unbeknown, I am sure, to themselves, they each compiled a comprehensive commentary on our shared lives, quite unable to resist the temptations scattered so liberally at their feet in the form of puns and verbal echoes, inversions, anagrams, homophones and all the other profligate glories of the repertoire. Nothing, it seemed, was forgotten. Here I would find, deftly masked, the reference to some still-simmering former grievance; there, in the interstices of a broken phrase, a furtive admission of unresolved guilt. There is no innocence in language.

And how did my friends react when confronted with this evidence? Sometimes with crass denials; sometimes with their own highly subtle exegeses of the clues they had provided; most often with long, rambling apologias whose transparent motives amused me no end. Indeed, I have found the exercise so compellingly instructive that I have decided to select appropriate passages from their letters as I proceed.

Every age has its characteristic literary form which answers to its needs of sense and sensibility – at one time the verse epic, at another the sonnet, the rhymed couplet, the novel. As this twentieth century nears its bloody, complex, fractured end, shall we not witness the apotheosis of the crossword puzzle? For it alone has the ability to make us whole. If, as I have argued, the two dimensions of surface and solution produce of themselves a third, does the subterranean clue not allow us to strike out into yet other, hitherto inaccessible, worlds? May this kaleidoscope of allusions not bring into being a very universe of thought and feeling? Teeming histories, vast geographies and deep, questing philosophies! Might not a single (admittedly highly remarkable) clue sum up an entire life?

I cannot pretend that what I offer here entirely meets such an ambition. Those to whom I have turned possess the usual human foibles, including partiality, dishonesty, vindictiveness and forgetfulness, as well as a mixed ability when it comes to compelling the English language to the strenuous demands of a crossword puzzle. I am, moreover, concerned not to encumber the reader with a surfeit of embarrassing personal detail. Reticence will prevail. Nevertheless, I believe that I may lay claim to a method which can be developed by others, until all that needs to be thought and said may be contained within one simple symmetrical grid and fewer than thirty clues.

Douglas O'Dale

ACROSS

1 Firm century by Kent opener – and a succession of others, apparently, well before lunch (4-4)
5 I break faulty copper with do-it-yourself bodge. Result – a cold bath! (3-3)
9 Dissociation of initially upper-class poet agitated about fanciful imagery (8)
10 Roll up to roll the girl, we hear (6)
12 Lightweight craft is overwhelmed in the main (5)
13 Dreadful pun – to wit, owl begins to sing! (3,2,2,2)
14 Tips the wink – and a nod, maybe (7,5)
18 Quarter a German army in the block – a frightening experience (6,1,5)
21 Low point: I succumb to uncanny display of force. Lunacy! (4,5)
23 Find within him a godlike, perfect form of life (5)
24 Shamefaced about sin, Falstaff's poison (6)
25 A little street-wise, breaks rules (8)
26 Creature threatened with extinction for ever and ever (3-3)
27 Play the Fool? (3,5)

DOWN

1 Universe of a hundred thousand scattered bones (6)
2 Furnished with Chambers, yet rarely finding poetic voice (6)
3 Retreat for the wounded – and ruled (3,3,3)
4 Mood pill can't remedy? Apparently so (3,9)
6 Restrict stuff included in crossword puzzles initially (5)
7 Engage treacherous fellow in wild duel – of the verbal kind (8)
8 Fiction that's false shan't pay! (8)
11 Ironic, for instance, that nobody does less to subvert a script than I (12)

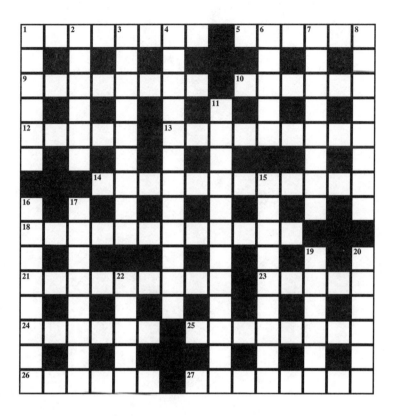

15 Garbled little account enthralls us. It is abnormally preoccupied with matters of conscience (9)

16 Continent to the letter, as before – causing pathological linguistic impotence (8)

17 Personal resolution does feel justified (4-2-2)

19 Plumb the depths of human tragedy for a spell (6)

20 Wary of the Almighty when mad dog fastens upon rear (3-3)

22 I'm at first accusative, then cry wildly – at last find grace (5)

ACROSS

1 Firm century by Kent opener – and a succession of others, apparently, well before lunch (4-4)

'Bravo!' writes the waywardly ebullient Dennis Millay. 'An opening to rival the Irish artificer and his ersewile mysterpose. Didn't he launch himself with that seminal *riverrun,* and doesn't your *cock-crow* match it for fecund significance?'

I should pay more attention to Millay's enthusiasms were his clues of a passable standard. 'Well before lunch' is the gravest weakness here, the continuance of the cricketing terminology being a jejune and risible excuse.

The whole thing is unforgivably quirky, albeit that several conventional abbreviations do come into play: 'firm' conjures up 'co' (for company); 'c' stands for century; and 'k' is borrowed from Kent (the first letter, or opener). 'Please applaud,' the man has the nerve to request, 'their happy manipulation into a sporting phrase.'

And what of the coda? The word 'apparently' properly warns the astute that there is trickery afoot, but what are these other centuries? The benighted solver will certainly hit upon the answer before he grasps the notion: 'c row', a row, or succession, of centuries.

'Eu-bloody-reka,' as Will Frome might put it in a rare classical allusion.

Cricket, mercifully, is still understood wherever Englishmen meet together. The classics are another matter. 'Eureka' one might just get away with, but the range is much diminished. Even the best puzzles have turned away from that rich store of learning to inhabit an arid mental landscape disfigured by growths such as (and I quote from some recent examples) quarks, memes, bytes and parsecs.

A parsec, according to my dictionary, is a unit for measuring the distances of stars, being the interval (about 19 billion miles) at which half the axis of the earth's orbit subtends an angle of one second. And the band, as my grandmother used to say, played Believe It If You Like.

While there is language, I suppose, there will for ever be crossword puzzles, but the genre demands a nurturing communal experience. In those halcyon days (but forgive me!) when I first compiled for the *Times*, my readers still shared an easy familiarity with Greek myth, with the authorized version of the Bible and the complete works of Shakespeare, along with much else already sucked into the obliterating depths of civilisation's swift ebb-tide. We shared a time, a place, a continuum of meaning. There was no straining to be understood. Eheu!

It is not difficult to envisage the day when, each retreated into his own private enclave, we have too little in common to sustain us in our allusive wit. Where shall we find a world-view to replace the one we lost? Surely not in all our fashionable isms; our desperate arts; our distrusted sciences.

A parsec is, of course, no more (and no less) real than Sisyphus with his boulder or the sweet siren voices tempting tethered Odysseus to his doom.

By far the best of the submitted clues was Doug Mailer's *Early birds*. Its stark, heart-stopping beauty, that elegant frugality, far surpasses Millay's dreadful effort, but the very perfection (the first word represents the whole solution, while the second refers to the comically mismatched *gallus* and *corvus*) sadly renders it immune to interesting criticism.

Something far more elaborate arrives from the pen of Lester Dunt: *Dawn to ring Labour about Tory infiltrations.* We must allow that the political surface is neatly contrived. Dawn is apparently a rebellious young lady of gentle breeding eager, for reasons we can only guess at, to ingratiate herself with members of the working class by betraying her own kind. Furthermore, the true nature of the riddle is adroitly masked, the code difficult to break. (Should we look to 'dawn' or to 'infiltrations' for the key to the solution?). If 'ring' instantly yields 'o', it is only after much hawing and havering that we place next to it ('to' being a rather weak signal) the letters 'krow' – labour about! – and complete the picture by inserting those intrusive Conservative Cs.

Dunt at first disavowed any personal resonance in this clue. It was a mere opportunistic fabrication. The words and ideas had fallen into place according only to the dictates of the solution. Great was the feigned surprise when I reminded him of a certain young lady of our acquaintance named Eve (the crepuscular counterpoint was striking) and a certain infiltration with memorable consequences. He allowed, at least, and at last, that there might be 'faint echoes':

*We were holy rustics all, christened by dewdrops
and drips from the thatches, confirmed in the*

unchanging rites of the changing seasons, our sacraments the biscuit-coloured filberts we greedily crunched, the elderberries that stained our lips purple-red through the simmering, shimmering expirations of those long and languorous summers. We knew petty wrong-doing in plenty but were ignorant of wickedness.

Life was savoured on the tongue, touched by the fingers, rubbed against the skin - an existence of unbroken sensation which, though sometimes painful, occasionally dangerous, never penetrated that vulnerable psyche of which we had no intuition. Slower than city boys, we had until then registered the presence of girls only as irritating sisters, spoilers of boisterous games, tellers of tales. They had no power that we were aware of, no capacity for turbulence.

Well do I recall that slumbering afternoon at harvest-time when we saw the carrier's cart stopped in the shade outside the doctor's house. There were four or five of us, stumbling heat-stupid along the lane, too weary to help in the fields, too aimless to do more than swat one another childishly with sticks and stalks.

'There'll be plenty visiting here!' old Sime guffawed, jerking his horny thumb at the house even as he flicked the mare into action with the reins. 'That's a right purty little lady.'

And, although we cared nothing for prettiness, curiosity sent us scrabbling on hands and knees through the dark, earth-smelling caverns sculpted by the roots of the thick-leaved trees bordering the garden. We crept to the hedge of glossy laurel and each tugged a little window for himself.

She was alone, stretched on the grass, the flimsy summer dress pulled up to brown her legs. That was all. We could scarcely see her face. Her fingers lazily pulled at the green shoots. Her toes were bare.

Even more wondrous than the stirring of a new consciousness, the eerie, certain premonition of an irreversible inner process, was the communal nature of its swift uncoiling. We crouched shoulder to shoulder, yokels at a peep-show, and were in that moment transmogrified.

The evidence is surely conclusive. I only wish that Dunt had avoided that smutty little joke at the end.

5 I break faulty copper with do-it-yourself bodge. Result – a cold bath! (3,3)

'Have you the memory,' enquires Will Frome, 'of that tremendous scrap with the wall-eyed London bobby? They styled him the Perilous Peeler. Blood and teeth from the very first round, and the water in the bucket was raspberry froth . . .'

Strange how the hard currency of one man's life is the devalued small change of another's. I confess that I strain to hear the rattle of coins in the tin.

'By the third you were neither seeing clear through the crimson haze. Every shake of the head sent a cascade of rubies through the heavy air.'

Frome's clue is marginally more artful than his prose. The faulty copper is a reversed PC, while the bodge involves the letters DIY. With the initial 'I', this produces *Icy dip*.

The surface meaning is more suggestive to me than Frome's elaboration of the subterranean. How forget the aching chill of our makeshift gymnasium above the White Hart? That old cracked-fingered Will was responsible for the uselessness of the boiler I can well believe. It certainly served as nothing more than a stand for bottles of linament and embrocation, and what faint heat we enjoyed came from the paraffin lamps which we eager, thin-vested novices would pump like manic galley-slaves those long winter evenings. At the conclusion we threw cold water over ourselves and briskly towelled our fevered flesh.

But the man's memory must be at fault in several

particulars. Surely the Board would have refused a certificate to any boxer with a wall-eye. In those early amateur bouts a fight would have been instantly stopped at the drawing of blood. We all wore gumshields, and I have no recollection of teeth being lost. Even that alliterative soubriquet strikes me as mistaken. Was my opponent not known as the Fearsome Flatfoot?

The local force had invested heavy money in their boy, and his gloves were weighted with it. Too much need and greed for his frame to carry.

Poor kid, he was floundering well before the end, flogged by the merciless demands of his backers as much as by your busy fists.

We were patching you up between rounds, stemming the blood, dashing the salts under your nose, bawling in your ear, and out you went swinging. Never knew a braver.

And yet you took it with a piece of trickery I'd never have thought to teach you. Desperation was feeding his unscrupulousness. He was using the head, banging it about your face. Twice you stepped back to appeal to the referee. No dice. Next time, back you stepped again – and then, before old Perilous could collect his wits, over the top of his droopy guard you went. He slumped in a corner and, though he struggled up, the referee waved him away and it was all over

The other trainer refused to accept it. He had far too much to lose. You could see him wildly eyeing the crowd at the end of each round, and now he was beside himself with fury – which was really fear. He was yelling at the referee, prodding him against the ropes.

I, of course, was tipsy with good humour, both for the victory itself and a sum of money won at very decent odds. I pushed through the mêlée to share the moment with you – but, you fighters! The rest of us were mere intruders, while the pair of you slipped into a long and sweaty embrace, like lovers, two against the world.

9 Dissociation of initially upper-class poet agitated about fanciful imagery (8)

No, this really will not do. It is a typical, and lamentable, example of Millay's stretching the conventions practically to breaking point.

The solution is *solitude*. I am prepared to grant a degree of wit in the choice of that word 'dissociation', an equivalent which clearly points the quill at a particular poet. I mean, of course, at T.S. Eliot, famous for the phrase 'dissociation of sensibility'. (He also wrote a few poems.) It is true, moreover, that Eliot the imagist detested the fanciful. But may the word 'idol' properly be clued by 'imagery'? I think not.

'Initially' prompts us to take 'U' for upper-class and 'TSE' for the poet (who is Millay's obsession, not mine); 'agitated' leads us to jumble them; 'about' reveals that other letters come between; and 'fanciful' indicates that the letters of 'idol' are likewise to be rearranged.

Millay's notes include a version which I believe I prefer, though he has heavily crossed it through. After 'poet' it runs: 'possessed by strange god'.

My contributor has an Eliot fantasy quite in keeping with other of his absurd interpretations of artistic achievements. He lacks, I shall explain, the slightest historical sense and regards any evidence adduced against his theories as so much quibbling. I have heard him argue, for instance, that Beethoven's Moonlight Sonata was so named in cock-snooking celebration of the fact that, while in the oppressive employ of the Elector of Cologne, he was by night supplementing his income fiddling with a gypsy combo in the shadier parts of Bonn. Similarly, Millay's story is that Handel's Harmonious Blacksmith was originally written to be played on a phalanx of especially tempered horseshoes by a hearty farrier with whom he was emotionally close. Unsurprisingly, my friend's explication of the smile on the face of the Mona Lisa is highly ingenious, although it need not detain us.

Concerning Eliot, Millay is for some reason in thrall to a (surely distorted) vision of the great man working in a London bank, a position he actually held but for a few early years. Here we see the outraged romantic in Millay, I fear, unable to envisage Euterpe wearing an orange rubber finger-stall.

That famous opening of *The Waste Land* ('April is the cruellest month . . .') is for Millay merely a symptom of Eliot's infection by scrofulous Mammon. 'The end of the tax year!' he cries emphatically. 'Horrendous paperwork and a rattling of slide-rules to calculate the effect of the Chancellor's new fiscal measures. All expenses claims in, please. All accounts finally totted. Overtime this evening, Mr Eliot!' It is as if the rest of the poem were simply a gloss on these mundane financial considerations. *Ash Wednesday*, in particular, gives Millay a field day:

It's getting on for three in the afternoon. You have to remember that it's a Wednesday: early-closing day. Nobody about. The great banking hall echoes with the footfalls of a solitary messenger making his sedate way across the marble floor, between the marble columns. Slowly edge the hands of the clock towards, Eliot perhaps muses, the positive hour. A pleasing phrase!

He sits upright behind the counter, collar stiff, tie meticulously knotted. Teach us to sit still! To one side of him, a pile of cheques neatly corseted by a rubber band. Next to them the scales with their burnished weights. Further over, tactfully concealed from clients, a short list of accounts which may not be drawn on. To his other side, a neat row of pens and pencils, a rubber, an inked stamp, a monographed pounce-box, perhaps, and (most important of all) his pad. The exposed page is all scribbled o'er with a camouflage of supposed additions and subtractions, but within . . .

Beetling that severe brow, flicking back that lick of swart hair over his forehead, Mr Eliot guiltily turns back the page. Oh, virgin whiteness! He reaches for his favourite pen, fastidiously removes the protector from his index finger and for a few seconds stares into enmarbled space. The words have been forming all day. He begins to write:

Because I do not hope to turn again

Comes a jangling crash and the pen, poised to continue, whips upwards like a jerked knee and is swiftly replaced on the counter.

'Blimey, what a day!' laments a cheery fellow still wearing his greengrocer's apron and busily unloading bags of coins from a slatted wooden

27

crate. 'Quiet as the grave until midday and then they call come with a rush. Thought I'd never get the place shut up.'

Our teller would like to smile but has forgotten the art. He weighs the coins, irritated fingers picking out copper which has found its way into the silver.

'Ain't seen yer before. New are yer?'

The slick of hair lowers itself marginally in affirmation.

'Not much of a job, is it? Still, I suppose it's a rung on the ruddy ladder. Got to be thankful for a job these days . . .'

Endless chatter; the eventful life and times of greengrocery; coins and more coins; at last the stamping of the receipt.

'Ta, mate. Keep smilin', eh?'

Teach us to care and not to care! Five to three. He picks up the pen. The mood has almost left him, so that he must needs fall into a light trance once more and begin again:

Because I do not hope

'Excuse me. Can't change a tenner for me, can you?'

How can he speak? His mind is far away, wherever poets take them. Three well-fed white leopards are already stretching under a juniper-tree several lines ahead. He pushes ten crisp notes across the counter. Receding footfalls.

Because I do not hope to turn

A bell rings somewhere deep within the marble tomb. Yes, it's three o'clock. Another day gone and not a line completed – or, as it later transpires, only three. (When writing's this difficult you don't waste a thing). Old Ezra was all for banking theories, but at least he contrived to have himself housed where pounds, shillings and pence never interfered with his creativity.

Notwithstanding that I have always found it futile to argue with Millay, I did look through the poem for evidence which would refute his weird gloss. Unhappily the poet himself does a grave disservice to his defenders at the opening of the last section. I suspect that Millay is keeping this ammunition up his sleeve for further battles:

Although I do not hope to turn again
Although I do not hope
Although I do not hope to turn

Wavering between the profit and the loss . . .

10 Roll up to roll the girl, we hear (6)

October was dwindling, droop-leaved and damp, and we scurried about the wood's edge and under the sycamores by the green for Guy Fawkes Night kindling. The bonfire was building well, a ramshackle wigwam which, apart from its routine superstructure of dead branches, incorporated withered tomato stems and potato haulms from the allotments, a mortally wounded mattress, two broken chairs and a sign reading 'Trespassers Will Be Prosecuted', which had long been a source of rancour on our lawless wanderings.

To all appearances a simple re-enactment of the annual custom, this year's event was different for us in a way we could scarcely admit to our own secret hearts. We busied ourselves with the preparations and said nothing about the girl. Yet we knew. We knew that each of us, returning home to hot cocoa and a vigorous wash behind the ears before bed, would enjoy long, langorous reveries in which a vision of Eve came to us, warm, smiling, willing to do whatever it was that girls did. This mysterious, sensual presence had disturbed, inspired us continuously from that day of our enchantment.

Our unformed desires would, we reasoned with the logic of ardent, untutored primitives, be sure to find satisfaction on the magical evening of November the Fifth. Since that first sighting, she

30

had practically disappeared from view, glimpsed but fitfully driving through the village with her well-to-do guardians or, again chaperoned, crossing the busy street while shopping in town; but the bonfire brought everyone together.

It was a clear, crisp night, the stars almost close enough to pluck from the ebony sky and use for sparklers. Knot of onlookers gradually fused into a crowd, and rags soaked in paraffin were pushed into the base of the bonfire and lit. Gouts of grey smoke pulsed from the great wooden pyramid. We cheered the first flames while anxiously watching out for a notable absentee.

'Where's . . . everybody?' asked gormless Bertie, blushing beautifully as he tried to strangle his question at birth.

'Where's who?' we all chorused, revealing our own desperate preoccupation even as we ridiculed his. 'Who're you waiting for, Bertie?'

'Dunno what you mean,' he blurted sullenly, picking up a stick and hurling it into the roaring inferno.

She came at last. Soft as silk, still as lake water, she observed the sputtering roman candles, the vivid eyeball-searing snowstorms, the shrieking, tear-away rockets, with an unexpressive detachment. This, of course, served only to intensify our fervour, and we drew as close as we dared, jostling, aching for a sign.

When a smouldering log rolled out of the fire between us she caught my eye for a second. Then

she became aware of the ogling gang and looked
away in what I took for scorn, and I felt a burning,
acrid shame.

Perhaps Dunt's shame should be reserved for the double crudity of his clue. The surface is undeniably distasteful, and no more needs to be said about it, but I am also unconvinced by the use of 'roll-up' to signal a cigar, or *Havana*. Surely the term can be applied only to a hand-made cigarette. The 'we hear' convention is tired but useful.

Among other submitted clues I most liked *Capital smoke!*, which neatly combines both meanings of the solution. And I least liked Millay's concoction: *City in which a Van Allen might live*. I am not over-enamoured of hidden-word clues at the best of times, since they smack of children's puzzle books, but this one seems particularly crass. The reference would seem to be to the distinguished American physicist J.A. Van Allen (indeed, Millay's note confirms this), but unless there is any record of his having lived in Cuba the surface clue is vacuous. I utterly reject Millay's story of the frayed belt and the subsequent conviction for indecent exposure.

A similar clue comes from Doug Mailer, and I break it up to demonstrate its decidedly choppy construction: *Crash a van at/centre of/town*. Its legitimacy is as dubious as its inspiration was obvious to me. Mailer needed little prompting:

In the spring of 196— received a letter from Seed,
an old university friend. This surprised me somewhat,

for he had long since moved abroad and, apart from the perfunctory sending of Christmas cards, we had not been in touch for several years.

His initial tone certainly gave no clue as to my friend's motive for writing. In a matter-of-fact way he outlined his recent career: he was something in the money markets; held a few directorships; owned a couple of houses, one in the city, another at a holiday resort; and so on. It was all fairly predictable.

Towards the end of the letter, however, I began to notice a change to a more urgent style. He reminded me that he had a son, Grant, whom I had not seen since he was about six years old. The lad, I was rather earnestly informed, had grown into a strapping young man of eighteen. There followed an encomium which even at first reading had a touch of desperation about it, as if my friend were trying to persuade himself as much as me.

All began to become clear when I read that young Grant was now a history student at Oxford, the town where I had my solicitor's practice. The first request made of me was that, without any inconvenience to me and so forth, I might keep an eye on his offspring, who was on his own in a strange country and was possessed of a slight (though only natural for his age, etcetera) tendency to waywardness. The second request was to represent the young man in court, where he was shortly to appear on a charge of reckless driving.

How could I refuse? I duly interviewed the boy,

who was considerably less than repentant, and argued his case with moderate success. As I recall, he received a small fine and a severe wigging.

So began a relationship which was to bring me the utmost inconvenience and pain .

12 *Lightweight craft is overwhelmed in the main (5)*

'But not in your case!' insists Will Frome.

The craft fashioned by the subterranean clue is a canoe which, having being overwhelmed, is rebuilt as *ocean*, hitherto known to poets and historians of an antique bent as 'the main'. (Crossword puzzles are nothing if not eclectic). This is satisfactory, but – hard as Frome tries – the surface is distinctly lack-lustre. Do we really care about the fate of this little vessel and its single occupant? One upturned skiff is much like another. Should we not have the circumstances suggested to us? Was the weather turbulent? How experienced was the canoeist? Did he appreciate the danger or, in any imaginable way, actually invite it?

Those long evenings skipping and jogging and pounding the bag! I never regretted a second because I knew you had the snap in your sinews, the cauldron in your belly. You had the pedigree.

A common misuse of the language among the sporting fraternity, for whom 'pedigree' often signifies nothing more than talent or, at most, an outstanding record of achievement. There was certainly no pugilistic tradition in my family. Furthermore, if I may be allowed to pre-empt Frome's frantic effusions on the subject, I myself had no ambitions whatsoever in this regard.

And you had a champion's grit in you from the first. Determination. Coaching you was a dream.

Do you remember how we worked on hooking off the jab? First the left jab itself, that iron piston hammering away, blow after blow, the softener. Then the surprise – that swift left hook, the destroyer. You had it perfected within a month. In-bloody-credible!

We took 'em by storm. They saw only this spindly wraith with neat footwork, and the bruisers reckoned they could smash their way through. Smash my arse! They couldn't lay a glove on you.

That night at the Sweeney Club, with all the toffs in their penguin suits puffing mile-long cigars over their trout and pheasant, I was setting you up for a tilt at the title. I'd pushed you into the merciless glare of the spotlights, a lamb led to ceremonial slaughter from the clubbing fists of Brian the Bermondsey Battler.

They've the good eye, those clients at the dinner clubs. Present them with the real thing and they recognise it before a round's up. There's no more eating or drinking then until the bout's over. Their glossy womenfolk are suddenly useless ornaments, completely forgotten. They shrink into the background and don't dare speak a word.

So it was on the night you taught poor punchy Brian what hooking off the jab was all about. The silence was so palpable it sweated. You slipped in and out of his shadow, and wup-wup-wup went that jab. An awed silence.

You allowed him nearly two rounds and then the hook sprang out of nowhere and he was gone. And you know what you said to me afterwards? 'I didn't feel it.'

Of course you don't feel the best knock-out punches. The timing and the tension are just right, and he goes as if you've shot him. But you said it like a complaint, as if you'd been cheated. 'I didn't feel it,' you said – as if you wanted some kind of violent spasm along your arm to complete the enjoyment.

13 Dreadful pun - to wit, owl begins to sing (3,2,2,2)

It is the female of the species *Strix aluco* which utters the cry commonly transcribed by our lexicographers (there are variants) as 'tu-whit'. The male is supposed to reply 'tu-whoo', and cultural conditioning is such that few Englishmen have heard the birds speak in any other accents, however much ornithologists may argue for 'kewick' and 'hoo-hoo-hooooo'.

The least adventurous of travellers will soon discover the puerile perfidy of the written word. Children in the French Midi recite a verse whose effects depend upon a rhyme with 'tee-vit'; a Corsican peasant will slit your throat rather than give ground over the unmistakable 'hrru-vich'; while I myself have held my tongue as haversacked German youths have paused in their nocturnal forest rambles to mimic the 'schee-whip' of the polylingual tawny owl.

My next encounter with Seed was in circumstances I later came to recognise as typical. One evening, long after I had retired to bed, the telephone rang. I was inclined to ignore it (with more good sense that I then knew) but its persistence at last overcame my resolve. I struggled into my dressing-gown, stumbled downstairs and muttered something illtempered into the mouthpiece.

There was no immediate response. I could hear

only a babble of voices, which suggested to me a particularly riotous party. Just as I was about to hang up, a slurred voice, very loud, spoke my name. The speaker was evidently the worse for drink.

Doug Mailer's clue is rather good, and not difficult to solve for those who know that to 'sing' is underworld argot (in the cinema and crime novels, at least) for spilling the beans. I must register disappointment, however, than an enticing paronomastic invitation has been ignored. The word 'begins' signals that the first letter of 'owl' is to be used (together with the preceding eight), so that the mayhem alluded to ('dreadful') produces *Own up to it*. Could Mailer really have found no use for the witty notion of 'owl's lieder'? Readers with five minutes to spare may care to complete the task themselves.

Young Seed (for it was he) airily summoned me to a country house some ten miles from Oxford. It was a demand which, in my anger, I found easy to resist. However, an older and altogether more authoritative voice now took over and, in somewhat austere tones, assured me that the matter was sufficiently serious as to warrant my intervention. Feeling the obligation to my distant friend, I reluctantly acquiesed.

Little evidence of former revelries remained by the time I arrived. A bright light burned in the hall. A few sheepish stragglers were taking their leave, eyeing me somewhat warily. My brain registered a sweet and heavy odour that I did not know.

My protegee was discovered lying flat on his back on the tiled floor of the conservatory. He wore a multi-coloured kaftan; there was a string of beads about his neck; and his hair, which had grown considerably since our first meeting, was tied behind in a ribbon. Although his eyes were open, he scarcely seemed to recognise me.

Seated next to the prostrate body was a man in his forties who, extending his hand to me, rose from the chair and introduced himself as Mr L—, the owner of the house. He explained that there had been a slight accident. Had I perhaps passed the ambulance? (I had not). One of the guests, a young man, had fallen from a balcony. It was possible that he had broken a leg. There was, it seemed, a degree of concussion. Mere horseplay, he insisted. Young Grant and the unfortunate guest . . .

Contrition for whatever part he had played in the escapade was not something I expected of Seed. I was, however, shocked by the merry laugh that now issued from his lips. 'He tried to fly,' he said, 'but he stopped to think. He betrayed his Zen.'

I asked whether the police had been called, and learned that they had not, 'in the circumstances'. It was then that I realised what should have been already obvious to me. Seed was not drunk, but under the influence of marijuana.

'You can fly, man,' he addressed me earnestly, sitting up and clutching my arm. 'Shall I show you how to fly? You can float away like a beautiful soap bubble - but first you have to relax and let go.'

14 Tips the wink – and a nod, maybe (7,5)

Is there something in the English temperament which thrills to the very notion of secrecy? I simply ask the question. My current general hosts, the American people, have little sympathy with the concept, and I find myself fervently in accord with them.

From my window, as I write, I have a view across a small lake, with a single boat bobbing, to a range of low hills. A hundred years ago, I am led to understand, the intervening tract of land was little more than a wilderness. Now I see orchards, farms and factories. Could a cautious, fastidious people have so transformed the landscape in but a few generations?

My particular host betrays all the robust qualities one would expect of a race of pioneers, from a lack of moral squeamishness to a distrust of intellectual niceties. To encounter this fine gentleman is to succumb to the theory of environmental conditioning. He displays a healthy disapproval of refinement and declares forthrightly that each man has a duty to act openly and honestly with his neighbour.

He would, I regret to say, find my own friends and colleagues devious and over-subtle. Moreover, had he the ability to understand my project, he would be not in the least surprised to discover how eagerly, and in what numbers, they flocked to provide clues for 14 Across. Alas, the quality is at variance with the quantity.

Will Frome's offering, given above, is the best of a very poor bunch. The solution is *Cryptic Clues*. 'Tips' stands for the complete answer, and the slang phrase 'tips the wink' provides a cunning enough smokescreen: the solver will have a little trouble fathoming quite where to focus his attention. In fact, the wink and the nod are but concrete examples of those coded intimations of the solution.

Selecting but a few of the many tendered clues for brief comment, I offer them to critical public gaze in order of increasing insipidity:

Freakish circus type – small type, short, deep wrinkles. We are supposed to envisage, and no doubt recoil from, a stereotyped dwarf figure. Let anyone fall a few inches below or rise a few inches above he norm and there will be those quick to ridicule his so-called freakishness. The small are at least attributed with vigour, cunning, gross sexual drives, knowingness, but the tall are merely figures of fun – gangling stick insects, uncoordinated, asexual, quixotic.

The clue is reasonably straightforward. The letters of 'circus type' mingle with 'lc', the short form for 'lower case'.

CCCP? Surely it disseminates coded information.
The initials are the greatest weakness, since we in the West always knew the late dismembered Soviet Union as the USSR. A ring of desperation, therefore. And do we really wish to perpetuate the tired myth of the sinister Red menace? Even my host nation has shown some signs of recovering from its chronic paranoia.

Are cross words spoken by those who fail to understand them?
Beta double minus at best. This is limp. We need a proper yoking of 'cross words' and 'crosswords': the puzzles, of course, cannot be spoken. This is bad art.

Subtle hints that newspaper chapel twists evidence.
Dennis Millay parades his customary self-satisfaction over a typically unsatisfactory clue. A chapel in the world of the British press is a union branch, but the 'twisting' of the publication and the crypt would be acceptable only if we could be expected to divine that 'IC' stood for the *Investors Chronicle*, a financial weekly published in London. This is intelligence too arcane, surely, even for devotees of the crossword puzzle.

Millay, inevitably, claims not only to be thoroughly familiar with this esoteric publication but to have written for it, and (with what unfeigned joy he relates it) to have once perpetrated a crass, punning joke in its stock market report: 'Look up your file copies for December, 1964,' he burbles, 'and you'll find reference to a completely fictitious engineering company, Cochan, Bull!'

From such imbecilities one would ask to be spared.

Cicely Crupt's Crafty Concealments.
Were a novel with this title to appear on my desk I should find it hard to resist peeking inside – or rather, if I am honest, balancing the spine in order to discover at which page the book fell open – but as a crossword clue it is quite ridiculous. I am convinced that nobody named Cicely Crupt ever existed.

Cultic Cyphers from Celtic Cyprus.
Similarly, one has to ask whether there has ever been any Celtic influence whatsoever on this much-ravaged Mediterranean island, where some three-quarters of the population are Greek-speaking members of the Eastern Orthodox Church and the rest are Turkish Muslims.

This bodes fair to be the smartest clue in the entire book. It has color and style. It was given me by someone who lives close to the place where I am penning this. What you do is shake up the letters of CELTIC CYPRUS. The CULTIC CYPHERS bit makes a neat echo.

True, Richard the Lionheart captured it in 1191, and there was British rule from 1878 until the blood-letting of the 1950s, but the lasting influences have always been local in origin – Greek, Assyrian, Egyptian, Roman, Byzantine, Arab in early times; Greek and Turkish in the modern era.

And why 'Cultic'?

18 *Quarter a German army in the block – a frightening experience (7,1,5)*

Lester Dunt's submission actually read 'a spiritual experience', but I have taken the liberty of amending it in the interests of coherence. How should the presence of a foreign occupying force (this, I take it, being the likeliest reading) arouse feelings of an other-worldly nature? This kind of sloppiness in compilers is rife, and I abominate it.

It is a decidedly fragmented clue. 'Quarter' gives us 'SE' (one of the four quarters of the compass); 'a German' provides 'ein'; and the army is a 'host'. Alas, the signal 'in' is imprecise: here it is the block, or 'gag', which is incorporated within the other letters rather than vice versa. The solution, therefore, is *Seeing a ghost*.

Dunt's army turns out to be nothing of the kind, but a few raggle-taggle prisoners of war. Dare I suggest that what he likes to call his spiritual impulses may, in fact, spring from a point a little on the farther side of what I believe modern jargon would term the mind/body interface?

School had broken up for Christmas, and there was a keen, electric magic in the air. We felt it vibrating if we paused for a moment between the kitchen, where the mince pies were breathing warmth and spices, and the living room, which reeked of resin and was transformed into a cavern of green shadows under a great green tree.

We had raided the loft for our everlasting home-made decorations – the Chinese paper lanterns, the golden baubles which hung from taut, glittering threads, the wooden fairy with her crumpled, tinselly wings. Mysterious parcels in bright paper had begun to appear at the foot of the tree, and we slily turned them to find the names of their recipients, feeling them all over to discover what they might contain.

Outside there were leaden skies and a perpetual frost. The gaunt hedgerows chattered metallically at the merest breeze. Tree trunks were gleaming iron. Standing water was frozen to stone, and we put on our boots and slid on it, uttering wild cries which were instantly turned to steam and rose from our chapped lips as insubstantial ghosts of themselves, whispy alter egos.

We ranged through the village on these chill days, disturbing the genteel, terrorising the neurotic, offending the upright, and were the very soul of boorish lawlessness. We were the awkward squad, dangerously demob-happy. Let decent folk beware! Whenever we approached the doctor's house, however, an unseen but imperious RSM would at once call us to order, straighten our shoulders, cow us into silence, have us practically marching in step. We would, as if on an order, synchronously swivel our heads and fix furtive eyes upon the enchanted castle in which our princess lay imprisoned.

'Can't see what's so special,' someone would assert, anxious to display his bruised individuality.

'Course not,' would come the quick agreement.
'Who said there was?'

46

'Don't know what you mean.'

'Anyway, it was you wanted to come this way.'

'Never was.'

'Was so!'

The spell momentarily lifted, we would hurl our liberated bodies into a bloodless fray, inchoate young men become brawling boys again.

Our hopeless communal mooning over the unapproachable Eve threatened to make motley fools of us all and would undoubtedly have led to some kind of disgrace had it not been for the Enemy Invasion, as the event was immediately and ever thereafter known. It came unannounced and miraculously restored to us our fierce, crass masculine dignity.

Bertie saw them first, as he was eternally to remind us. 'Flamin' Jerries!' he gasped. (It was a veritable gasp). 'Bloomin' 'ell, look!' And we gawped as the cart rumbled by, old Sime's face triumphantly expressionless, half a dozen downcast men huddled together behind him, silent.

How did we know they were Germans before anyone had so much as given a hint of their arrival? We were certain from the very first. There was something about the set of their heads, and a dejection proper to their wretched station. We waited until they were safely distant, then shook our fists, barked uncompromising obscenities and spat noisily on the rock-hard earth. We held an earnest council of war as if the fate of the nation depended upon our deliberations.

'We'll mount a guard,' said Sid.

'Armed guard, day and night,' threw in Dennis. 'I'll pinch our spare breadknife.'

'And my Dad's cut-throat,' crowed Johnny, with the air of a cardsharp producing an ace. His father was safely away at the front.

Our vigilance was tireless if not, for lamentable practical reasons, a round-the-clock affair. The men were billeted at the largest farm in the village, and we would watch them stumbling out of the house in the morning, dressed in identical heavy coats, caps and mittens, in order to undertake such tasks as the weather would allow. They would stagger into the byres under ragged, flaking bales of straw, clean out the cattle stalls, exercise the steaming horses, tugging at the lead reins with a nervousness which suggested they were unused to animals.

At first they were simply The Enemy, sinister figures who might at any moment open a hidden trapdoor in the ground and beckon a thousand of their compatriots from the evil depths to overrun first our village, then our market town, finally the whole country. As time passed, however, we invented more believable fantasies, chose names and created individual histories for men whose characters became transparent to us even at the cautious distance from which we obsessively observed them.

Fritz, who was heavily tall, who flung his arms wide as he spoke and whose knuckly gutturals carried half a mile, was clearly an opera singer.

Helmut, who scampered about his duties, seldom uttering a word, must be a schoolteacher: he reminded us of a trousered Miss Plimpton, even though it was impossible to tell whether he had the same three stiff hairs sprouting from a wart on his chin. Kurt was a doctor (the style with which he smoked his wisps of cigarettes, like Dr Farnworth) and Carl (an easy authority) a village bobby.

Our official attitude to these poorly adapted creatures, beached on a cold and inhospitable shore, was one of unequivocal contempt. They were The Enemy and they had, moreover, managed to get themselves caught. If, privately, any of us allowed himself the indulgence of a stray sympathetic feeling it was never allowed to show. We devised endless stratagems, not only for plotting their every move, but for aggravating their pitiful condition through a regime of petty insults and ambuscades.

A week before Christmas the snow came. For a few hours it drove in from the east, thick and clinging, piling up against the windows, creating strange humps and bumps in the garden where the compost heap was and the log pile, an upended bucket and (trouble in store) an overcoat which one of my brothers had thrown off during play and forgotten.

Then the wind swung round to the south and the flakes became absent-minded wanderers, stupidly unable to make up their minds whether they were going up or coming down. The sky lightened. We tugged on heavy woollen socks which cramped our toes inside our wellington boots and ventured into a new world of fluffy booby-traps, plump, rounded contours and confused perspectives. We made deep Yeti-tracks in the snow and felt like the first, wild inhabitants of the planet.

One iridescent morning, with a ruby sun rising above flat cloud layers of pink and lilac, we huddled under an improbable halo of condensation and watched a carriage making its way towards the farm. The two horses trod gingerly, and their nervous slitherings took all our attention until we saw, perched beside her guardian on the front seat, our fair goddess, her hair bejewelled with gleams reflected from the snow.

'Look out!' cried Bertie instinctively.

He had voiced our collective apprehension: she was about to fall into alien hands, hands which would stop at nothing, whatever that meant. We had to save her.

'Someone's got to get in there and see what happens,' urged Sid as the carriage negotiated the rutted track and passed through the farm gates.

An uneasy democracy, we habitually cast lots at moments like these. Sid trawled in the snow with his large, capable hands and came up, red-fingered, with a clutch of twigs. He hid them behind his back and we each came forward, closed our eyes and stretched round him to take one. I drew the shortest.

'We'll give you,' Sid calculated, 'half an hour, then we'll come looking for you.'

'Good luck,' said Johnny.

'Don't get captured!' called Dennis.

The route to the yard was pre-ordained. The spiny hawthorn hedge had been breached long since, as had a section of rotten timbering in a corner of the cowshed. The wood was slimy against my palms as I clambered through.

Inside, smothered by shadows, I heard the steady chewing of the cattle, an army of teeth on the march to nowhere. Groping my way forward I felt the rounded belly of a heifer hard against my hand, inhaled the dust stirred by restless hoofs, sniffed the acridity of dung mulched with foetid hay, kicked against an aluminium bucket, which slopped something heavy and cold on to my foot. It was a world of every sensation but sight, and I was as a newborn thing, confused and atremble, deliciously molested by touch and taste and smell.

Then I blinked and she was there, standing in the weak winter light at the open doorway, a ghostly vision seen through the steam which rose from the feeding beasts.

Outside, the prisoners were bustling about their tasks. I could see them through the slats in the wall. She was watching them pass to and fro, a little smile on her lips. Her hands were deep in her pockets against the cold, and every so often she would stamp her feet. I was soft as a snowflake with love.

Could I rescue her? Would she follow me through the shed and the hawthorn hedge to safety? But even as I began to rehearse my lines she made a sudden dash outside.

I peered through the wall. Silent Helmut was bent under a hefty sack, and his cap lay before him on the snow. Instead of fleeing from The Enemy she bent her knees, took up the cap and held it out to him.

'Run!' I wanted to yell. 'Before it's too late!'

He took the cap and fitted it back on his head. They exchanged words I could not hear. Then his free hand took one of hers and raised it to his lips. She blushed.

Helmut, reborn, took the sack with both hands and continued across the yard, while Eve, her cheeks still flushed, stood smiling in his wake.

21 Low point: I succumb to uncanny display of force. Lunacy! (4,5)

'To be precise,' asserts Will Frome tenaciously, 'to a scrawny little bleeder you should have been off within a single round. Des-bloody-picable, if you ask me.'

The humble domestic cow is as much a victim of aural convention as the poor tawny owl. In England she moos. The 'point' in this clue refers to the compass ('n') so that the first part of the solution is *moon*. The strange power is 'mana', engulfing the first person singular pronoun to create *mania*.

Right from the bell you were jaded, the feet not skipping, the hands drooping low. I was bellowing through air heavy with sweat, but you let him come at you, and his gloves were grazing your forehead till it was red raw.

At the end of the first there was a little nick under one eye, and I slapped on old Will's special embrocation, the used tea leaves with water, which wasn't strictly legal but which patched you up for another three minutes.

But it wasn't in you that night of defeat and disgrace. We were only halfway through the second when he brought one up from basement level and down you went – not only down but blacked out for a second or two, so that we had a date with the medics and a compulsory lay-off into the bargain.

We carried you away for safety's sake and laid

you down in the dressing room, and all the while
that I'm fuming at myself for making the match and
at you for how you've performed, guess what you're
doing. You're lying there with a big contented smile
on your face, as if being knocked unconscious was
some sort of privilege and you'd like to do it again.

Millay sends something eccentric: *Madness initially*
makes obscure officer national monument, acting nobly
in Antarctica. We are ('initially') to take the first letters of
the last nine words: hence the inordinate length of the
clue.

The reference, of course, is to the ill-fated British
Antarctic Expedition of 1911–12, a subject which brings
out the worst in Millay. He shares, I regret to say, the
contemporary urge to besmirch every good reputation.

'Note,' he admonishes in schoolmasterly tones, 'that
Captain Scott himself provided the rationale for
transforming his failure into a triumph with the
vainglorious promise "to go forward and do our best for
the honour of the country without fear or panic".

'We may salute Amundsen and his team, but – runs the
question which is never, quite, asked – would they have
known how to suffer without whimpering? Would they
have died like men? (Very likely, but we shall never
know). Yet perhaps even a stoically accepted death would
have been insufficient without that madness of our
obscure officer which ensured the expedition its place in
mythology.'

It was, readers will know, an act of sacrifice, not
madness. Captain Laurence Oates of the Inniskilling

Dragoons, crippled by frostbite, voluntarily walked out into the blizzard and certain extinction in order to save his colleagues.

'Call it sacrifice if you will,' consents Millay. 'These are delicate matters, but is it ever admissible for a man to take his own life? Granted, there may be occasions on which it seems a noble or dutiful act, rather than simply a sweet release. But is it any the less a monstrous self-indulgence?

'If we flinch from taking another man's life, how can we think to snuff out our own? What, in any case, do we mean by the possessive adjective? How dare we presume?'

23 Find within him a godlike, perfect form of life (5)

It was my misfortune to run into Grant Seed in The Broad one Saturday some few months after the marijuana episode. I had made discreet enquiries to satisfy myself that there were to be no untoward consequences arising from that piece of tomfoolery, and had ascertained that the youth with the broken leg was not to instigate legal proceedings.

Nonetheless, I continued to regard Seed as a potential source of great affliction, and was several times on the point of taking up the pen and confiding my fears to his father.

On this occasion I was caught off guard, a fact which I ascribe not only to the abruptness of our meeting but to the altered nature of his appearance.

From Doug Mailer (who seems to favour them) comes another hidden-word clue, and a straightforward one at that. Who will need more than a few seconds to lure *imago* from its obvious hiding place?

The belief that the imago represents the last stage of insect life is amusingly anthropomorphic, as if the largest form of the creature (which we are most prone to admire) were its acme. The truth is that reproduction in the insect world is a circular affair. Consider those moths which are born without the capacity to feed, whose function is simply to lay eggs and die. Is the process finished with that death? Clearly not. One might as well argue teleologically for the pre-eminence of the caterpillar.

The change was palpable, if somewhat difficult to characterise. The weather was cold, and he had on a loose woollen hat, but I could tell that his hair was much shorter than before. He wore, for the first time in my company, a tie. These were trivialities, however. The real difference was a bright, almost feverish, intensity of manner.

Before I knew it I had agreed to accompany him to a 'spiritual happening' somewhere 'just off' St Giles. He would, he assured me, detain me for only half an hour. In the event we followed street and alley for about fifteen minutes and were then involved for upwards of two hours in the business I am about to describe.

I was to some extent prepared for the experience by Seed's weird monologue during our walk. He talked of karma, of ectoplasm, of divine rays of light, and with such an incontrovertible earnestness that I could only nod my head from time to time as an indication that I understood. In fact I was beginning to fear for the lad's sanity.

As we approached the house (large, detached and Edwardian) he took my arm and whispered hoarsely: 'It's a great honour to be invited here.'

The door was opened by an unsmiling Oriental. Inside there was a pile of boots and shoes, which we were invited to augment with our own. Seed at this moment removed his hat, revealing, to my dismay, a head completely shaven.

In our stockinged feet we padded into a room such as one uses while waiting to see a doctor or dentist, save that its decorations were in the eastern style, with ivory buddhas, a bamboo screen, a burning taper and so on.

There were chairs around the walls. Perhaps a dozen people had preceded us, and they sat staring into the space ahead of them as if it contained something visible to their eyes, although certainly not to mine. I was relieved to notice that most of them were untonsured.

Seed pressed his lips to my ear: 'In a little while,' he said, 'we shall be admitted to the divine presence.'

My expression must have been sceptical, for he immediately launched into a whispered account of the sect and what it believed, to such effect that I resolved to send that letter to his father without delay. Young Seed, in short, appeared to have not the slightest grasp of reality. His waywardness, his irresponsibility, his new-found 'religion' – all, it suddenly became clear to me, were manifestations of the same malady.

A bell rang. We were ushered along a corridor and into a large hall richly decked out with tapestries, lamps, densely woven carpets and similar exotic paraphernalia. The place reeked of incense. At the far end there was what I can only describe as a throne, and on it, in a scarlet robe, sat a fat old Oriental gentleman making signs with his fingers.

We were all obliged to fall to our knees, Seed no doubt in a state of bliss, though I was very far from being so, whereupon the divinity began to chant something unintelligible which rolled on and on and on and seemed to have no ending.

24   *Shamefaced about sin, Falstaff's poison (6)*

At last! I was beginning to wonder when I should flush out the ineffable Goethe. This is his very first clue. He must have been biding his time.

'I'd have preferred *po*-faced,' he remarks in his customary insolent tone, 'since it fits the case rather better, don't you think? But the pudeur is real enough.'

The 'case' is myself. Readers will have gathered that Goethe is not the spirit of the famous German literatus, called up from the vasty deeps. He is a friend of Millay's rather than of mine, an old acquaintance with whom I share little but bitterly-contested memories. Being gratuitously offensive is his metier. My nickname for him, which happily stings, refers solely to his would-be, but painfully non-existent, understanding of the human condition, an accomplishment for which I take the great author-sage to be a paradigm.

'You, natch,' (why must he resort to slang and other low expressions to no evident purpose?) 'could never comprehend why Shakespeare's great knight should draw our sympathy, let alone our awed admiration. What are spontaneity and robust appetite to you but poisonous sins?'

Little would be gained from pointing out that the Bard's treatment of his character is severe. Goethe (*my* Goethe, that is) would either take Shakespeare himself to task or encourage his friend Millay to scribble a ludicrous sub-Bradlerian defence entitled 'How many hangovers had Sir John Falstaff?'. The crude fact is that the man has a fixation about my sobriety and self-control. Are these to be regarded as vices in our modern times?

I shall pause for a memory. A group of little boys, which includes Goethe and myself, stands silently before a cradle scene in the chancel of a parish church. It is an evening service, and low lights and candles create an intimate atmosphere for a children's performance of the Christmas story. We are wise men and shepherds. Mary gently lays her baby on the hay. Joseph stoops to gaze tenderly upon his infant son. Whereupon one of our number emits a blaring eructation which reverberates throughout the congregation and seems to threaten the very foundations of Christendom.

The perpetrator was Goethe, whose face reddened only from the effort of controlling wild laughter, while mine burned with embarrassment and a nameless fear.

'Not the least of your problems,' diagnoses Dr G., 'is an inability to confront the world of adult emotions in which shame might conceivably be appropriate. Why blush for the peccadilloes of our youth? Why rehearse old misdemeanours when there are fresh ones to commit?'

There are doubtless several ways of answering this complacent degeneracy. I shall merely content myself with reflecting that a sense of shame is the only decent response to some of Goethe's own 'misdemeanours', the which I would blush to recount.

But to the clue: to solve it we need to know that 'What's your poison?' is a formula for asking what someone would like to drink; and that Falstaff's particular favourite was sherris-sack, or *sherry*. (To sin is to err, while the shamefaced are shy.) As a clue, I have to concede, it is satisfactory. In terms of its relevance it is pathetic.

'The thumping irony is that the very censoriousness which leads you to lambast the sins of others blinds you to the multiplicity of your own. We're invited to admire the surface brilliance of the word-spinning O'Dale in the hope that we'll ignore the crawling can of worms for which it's a desperate cover.'

25 A little street-wise, breaks rules (8)

'Rules being for you,' the unquenchable Goethe continues, 'however rigid, however undifferentiating, the sole guide to behaviour, no matter what the nuances of circumstance. How often have I witnessed your deference to mere propriety, even when . . .'

But this is folly. The clue refers to a particular incident. Goethe's incursions are not only overbearing but otiose.

Next time I saw you with the gloves on I could hardly believe my peepers. It was Spring Fair time on the heath, and I was up there with a few of my mates, out rousting.

Course, I couldn't resist the boxing booth, could I? You could hear old Colly Bradshaw calling his wares from near a mile off – 'Come and see the heavyweight champion of Africa! He's big, he's black and he's never been beaten! Where's the local man who'll fight him?

Frome is to be commended for a deft use of obfuscating punctuation. The little street ('st') is followed by 'astute', which 'breaks' to give *statutes*.

It was a packed marquee and we had to brawl our way in. And who did I first see when I got inside? Yes, you – up in the ring, pulling on gloves with this supposed champion of Africa.

'Come on down out of there!' I yelled, but

63

everyone was shouting something or other. I could have recited the Lord's Prayer and no-one would have looked twice.

Course, he was no champ. For that matter he didn't look a real heavyweight and I doubt he'd been nearer Africa than the Bristol docks. But he looked mean enough, and you were still under the medics. How am I supposed to rescue your reputation while you're scrapping with riff-raff at fairgrounds?

We elbowed our way close to the ring, about half a dozen of us from the club, all pretty handy ourselves, and I can tell you we'd already had a skinful so we were bursting for some action. Colly saw us quick enough and he didn't look too happy. He had a habit of fingering his flattened ear when he was worried, and now he was practically tugging it off.

He rang the bell and you came forward, innocent as you like, expecting to touch gloves, and as you raised them in true Gentleman Jim fashion this black guy naturally swung hard underneath and drilled a hole in your midriff.

We hollered the place down as if we'd never seen such a dirty trick in our lives, but we knew all that was coming to you, and I was half glad of it because you were such a silly little fool to get taken in by it.

He drove you back into a corner, and – what a surprise! – it was the corner with the loose boards, and you stumbled off balance so he was able to get in close with his elbows and smash a few tasty punches into your face.

And next you rolled on the ropes in expert style to escape him, only the ropes were slack and you collapsed through them, and while you're hanging on for grim death he's flailing at you with great haymakers and there's blood running from your nose and over your eyes and I'm knowing that here's the sad and bloody end of a promising career.

26 Creature threatened with extinction for ever and ever (3-3)

Seed père, despite his request for my assistance in guiding young Grant through life's turmoil, responsed to my letter with marked detachment. I formed the impression that he had all but given up on the miscreant.

He begged my continued watchfulness, but in terms which suggested that his expectations of the lad were low. It was a judgement with which I found myself obliged to concur.

'Isn't this a futile exercise?' demands Goethe, as if he were a party to the experiences Mailer describes. 'Why the persistent pretence of false significations?'

But the 'signification', if I understand his own brand of pretentiousness, will emerge only when the tale is told.

'On the contrary, my poor blind friend: we shall need an interpretation. May I volunteer myself for the task?'

Were such an exegesis required, Goethe is the last person to whom I should entrust it.

'Because I might too readily tease out those potent (if I may borrow from a certain poet) objective correlatives? Because I understand the language you speak better than anyone? Believe me, it's far better to employ a sympathetic help-meet than have some malicious hack concoct a malevolent stew of barbarous, technicolour and all-too-plausible lies.'

I had expected that my letter would be regarded as confidential, but that this was not the case became obvious the instant I next encountered young Grant, who greeted me with an unbecoming truculence.

Since he had the temerity to launch into his crude animadversions on my own front step (having, moreover, disturbed me while listening to music) my inclination was to close the door in his face. He, however, would not allow it, putting his shoulder to the door and striding through the entrance lobby and into my sitting room, all the while berating me for my furtive tale-telling.

He was agitated to such a degree that I rather expected physical violence to ensue, but once his wrath was spent it was a very different Grant Seed who all but fell upon me.

I cannot applaud this clue, which refers to the weird Malagasy *aye-aye*, a creature which taxonomists have reluctantly agreed to class as a lemur but which displays features allying it with quite different beasts: ears like a bat's for sensing the crepitations of insects deep within the recesses of trees; teeth like a beaver's for tearing away the bark; a tail like a squirrel's for balance as it springs from branch to branch; and, hideous and terrifying, a long, arched, skeletal finger on each hand, tipped by a vicious claw.

One can have no quarrel with 'for ever and ever', but the first part of the clue is surely too general, even if sadly accurate. (The alleged balefulness of the poor animal has led to its persecution by the natives, whereas other lemurs are regarded with a touching reverence.) A compiler, after all, possesses every last scrap of relevant information, whereas potential solvers necessarily begin in utter ignorance, and he has a duty to be fair.

His eyes were wide and brimming with tears, and the hands which he held out towards me were imploring rather than hostile in intent. I took him by the elbows and sat him in an armchair, advising him to calm himself. He was shaking very badly.

'Can't go on,' he was moaning desperately over and over again. 'Can't go on like this.'

I poured a large, neat scotch and attempted to put the glass to his lips, but he pushed it away distractedly.

'Listen, old man,' I said, 'you'd better tell me what this is all about.'

'Shall *I* tell you what it's all about?' persists Goethe, with an air of obscene knowingness. The answer, frankly, is 'No, thank you'.

Between pitiful sobs, Seed began to tell me of his estrangement from the exotic oriental sect which I had so closely observed.

Whether he had offended in some way or had simply ceased to believe I could not at this stage determine. Certainly the poor fellow felt himself cast into some form of outer darkness although, ignorant as I was of such matters, it struck me that his fear was more appropriate to an apostate of a western, rather than an eastern, religion.

'Surely,' I reasoned, 'there must be a way back if you truly desire it?'

But no: this apparently was not the case. A door had closed behind him and there was nothing ahead but an inexpressible void. The Divine Light, he told me, was all that had saved him from total obliteration. Now he was fast disintegrating.

27 Play the Fool? (3,5)

'Do let me guess,' mocks Goethe. 'We're to have more country matters here. More adolescent tremblings. Plenty of foolishness, no doubt, but definitely not of the harmful variety. Far less uncomfortable than the real thing, wouldn't you say?'

I rather suspect that he would like to write the story himself, but lacks the courage.

'Who are you to talk of courage, who dresses all his facts as fictions?'

One spring day of catkins and sweet sunlight I stumbled between tall grasses at the wood's edge, my grey flannel trouserlegs clutched by entangling briars, my trespassing heart ensnared by love.

A lengthy chapter might be written on the use of the interrogatory symbol in crossword puzzles. I may yet furnish an addendum. The solution here is *Act crazy*, the capital F reinforcing the stage direction, as it were, of 'play' to indicate a theatrical context. What, therefore, does the question mark signify, it being redundant so far as plain sense is concerned? It implies, surely, that this is but one way of interpreting the solution – the more straightforward image which it evokes being not a well-rehearsed action skilfully creating an effect but the idiocy of someone who, for whatever reason, has lost all control. I suppose the American flavour of the phrase (we should surely write 'act crazily') only reinforces this interpretation.

'Are such niceties supposed to advance human understanding to appreciable effect? Or are they but another obfuscating device?'

She was gathering bluebells. Her bare white arms were flecked with tremulous shadows, as if a cloud of gauzy butterflies flitted about her. She was dancing light to me, and spring sap; she was fresh green shoots, pert, playful breezes, the fragrance of cow parsley – and when she stooped to pull the milkwhite stems, a glimpse of thigh above the secret cleft of her knee melted my brain and I reeled with a delicious giddiness.

'And at a safe distance,' remarks Goethe, displaying his customary asininity.

His own clue (*Statute broken – behave irresponsibly*) is clearly meant to annoy, but its very ordinariness prevents any hurt. The use of 'broken' for the state of madness is archaic, though I suppose the former meaning still maintains a tenuous toehold in the cracked surface of what we know as crazy paving. In any event, this offering fails to merit further consideration.

'Which is to say that you find it dangerous.'

How so?

'For its intimations, natch. For where it leads and you don't dare to follow.'

As she turned to retrieve a fallen flower she seemed to see me, though I crouched in the undergrowth like a frightened hare, my heart

*beating louder than the grandfather clock in our
parlour and ten times as fast.*

*Cradling her bouquet, she padded along the
twisting path through the beech trees, climbed over
the stile and dropped into the lushness of the
meadow, where drifting bees sucked at the clover
and a thousand nameless winged things hummed
and sang amid the trefoil and the cowslips, the
buttercups and cuckoo flowers.*

*There was no cover. I followed fifty yards
behind, dreading that she might notice me, longing
for the intimacy of a backwards glance.*

Perhaps, I say, it is less a question of fear than of tact.

'Tac*tics*,' he counters. 'Same root, different inflorescence.'

But what kind of a world would it be, I wonder, if we
dropped our modest pretences? Which of us could survive
such a crude directness, so unshadowed an honesty?
Would the braggart Goethe himself enjoy being stripped
of his camouflaging secrecies?

'Now we're talking business! Do I hear the hint of a
threat? Come, come – try me! Do I dare to eat a peach?
I'll swallow the very stone! Tell what you know about me
and be damned.'

However sincere he may sound, I do very much doubt
whether, for all his bluster, the fellow would tolerate the
gentlest lifting of the veil. It is, after all, unnatural to wish
one's own exposure.

'But to watch you making a poor fist of it would be a
delight, old mate. I challenge you! Spill the beans about
me. Tell the worst you know.'

Should such things ever be acknowledged save at the very gates of Heaven?

'*Hell*, old thing! Let's not kid ourselves – I know where I'm going. Don't think to spare me. Just write it all down. I absolve you of any charge of malice. I'll swear that I browbeat you into it.'

A tale once told can never be unsaid.

'An act of the greatest daring, therefore. Only your second ever and, who knows, perhaps the most fulfilling. Your finest hour. I know you've got it in you. Take up that pen!'

As if, in any case, we could hope to know anything of value about another soul.

'Or our own, my dear friend. Or our own. We merely trawl for intimations.'

In obliterating depths.

'Which tempt our timid skimmer of the surface even as he trembles with fright, is it not so? Enticing him with visions of soft green caverns safe beneath the tug of the waves, where the tides do not reach and the only sound is the siren song of the whale . . .'

DOWN

1 Universe of a hundred thousand scattered bones (6)

It was through the lens of a telescope that he formed those indelible, those life-staining attitudes which were to bring him at the last, through a cluster of trials, to the brink of a reckless self-destruction: to be precise, though the stark and shocking perspectives afforded by that first crude three-inch refractor thrust upon him by wheezy Uncle Mory.

This was on the occasion of his ninth birthday, spent like all its exhausting, stifling predecessors solely in the company of adults, powerful, garrulous, all-knowing adults, pressing all their weight of experience upon his compliant head.

'Here, boy,' commanded his mother's brother through a gasp, holding out what seemed to be a shoebox but which, after careful, mannerly opening, proved to contain a long metal tube, several lenses of varying specifications, a small tripod and assorted brass fittings. 'Keep you out of mischief.'

Whereupon they all closed upon young Goethe, enshadowing, engulfing, and instructed him in the correct assemblage of the thing in a babble of confusing, contradictory tongues, remorselessly, intimidatingly, until Uncle Mory himself had to reach down and take the parts in his large, white, plump hands, pushing and screwing and tapping until at last it stood complete, and the company laughed and clapped and told him what a lucky lad he was.

Here was his mother, her downy face close, smiling her love, that bony, unanswerable nose, the dark, swift eyes, the hair always frothing about her face. She willed him to be grateful. He was grateful.

Since the weather was fine the magical instrument was set up on the lawn, between the rhododendrons and the ornamental pond, and angled to entrap the rays of the low February sun until the glowing disc appeared on a sheet of card and it was just possible to make out a dingy sunspot or two near its periphery.

This sport over, they found the highest part of the garden and, visually skipping a mile of fields to focus on the main street of the next village, were delighted to make out the names on the fronts of the shops and the time on the church clock. Passers-by were named, occasioning much clamorous speculation as to their furtively conducted business.

Eventually, reluctantly, they left him to gaze at what he would, yet every so often, as the conversation dragged, one of them would stroll over and, after a theatrical stoop and a placing of bunched fingers across one eye, chuckle loudly over something seen or, more likely, imagined,.

His own preference was for the detail of a less distant elm leaf, deeply veined and trembling, almost graspable, richly individual in the chance framing of the lens. He ached to touch the beauty of its completeness. There was, for this moment, no other leaf on earth, or this was every leaf.

But the true and dangerous magic of the telescope, as he was very soon to discover, lay beyond its prodigious magnifications, impressive though they seemed to his untrained eye.

He did, indeed, wonder at the multiplicity of the constellations as, evening come, he sat in the darkness of the heavily-curtained attic room peering intently through the eyepiece while his uncle fussed, lectured, leaned across to squint and adjust, all the time improvising rich harmonies with every laboured breath. He did marvel at the definition of the craters stippled across the face of the gibbous moon.

'More than a thousand million years old, and some a hundred miles across. Will you remember that? See the mountain ranges and the seas, which are *not* seas but vast dry plains . . .'

All this, however, was new learning acquired in the traditional manner, from earnest instruction overbearingly imposed upon him. He absorbed such facts rapidly, without great effort. He was a bright lad, well spoken of at school. It was only when his uncle withdrew, had returned downstairs, and he sat alone at the telescope, that he felt his inner vision blur, felt his perspectives shift as they were to remained shifted for ever.

What was he looking at? At that time he had no knowledge of the heavens, so that we can only make a guess, though an informed one. We know that the room faced north, for instance, Moreover, he became aware that the stars were not uniformly white, as he had previously supposed. He contrasted one which flared crisply, inviolably pure with a near-companion that was (he could scarcely believe it and checked the lens) a deep, soft orange. Might this have been Aldebaran, perhaps, or even Pollux? Both are plausible, but I think not. He would surely have first picked out a striking constellation before turning the telescope upon its brightest members. I believe that in this way he tracked the brilliant stars of Orion until his right eye came to rest on the glowing ball of Betelgeux.

He focused upon Betelgeux and accepted its reality. That, I surmise, must have begun the process. A star, all the stars, became at that moment real. It was not, I stress, the magnification which brought about this realisation: a poor amateur telescope can make little of an object 350 light years away, however bright. It was the meditation, the fixing of his attention, in the darkness and the silence, upon its undeniable physical existence.

Did he not already know that stars were real? He had accepted it but he had not experienced it. The two kinds of knowledge are distinct, discrete. The stars had been emblematic, decorative, unknown. Now they were known.

The sense of their cold otherness must have followed almost as part of the same sensation. The stars were as real as he was, yet they were no part of his life, nor he of theirs. They were estranged. They were made of different stuff. Nothing connected.

All this he cannot have reasoned at his young age, but felt as a sudden chilling of the skin. As he swivelled the tube, slowly, tremblingly, he passed from one star to another across vast black wastes, empty voids which, too, must be as real and as wrapped in utter otherness – dead matter doomed to circulate for ever, unless it burned away or smashed or fused or exploded, in which case the new dead matter would spin away, hurtle on its meaningless journey, elements and gases, insensate, unregistered, for ever and ever, without end, without purpose.

At this moment, floors below, his mother laughed.

He could not deny the reality of what he had seen. He could not deny its implication. What was it that he shared with the stars, with their wandering planets, with the elements and the gases? What was it that gave them all, himself included, equal validity?

Existence. That he, too, existed. Nothing more.

He glimpsed, in short, and with a dreadful clarity, the barren futility of mere existence and that he himself was inextricably a part of it. For solace, perhaps, he brought back into view the ruddy warmth of Betelgeux. It offered only its otherness, and in recognising that otherness he understood his own, understood that he was mere matter among other matter, that he was as necessary as a wisp of gas from the smallest crater of a dwarf star hidden at the far side of the galaxy. This is a poor rationalisation of what, fleetingly, he must have experienced with the full force of all its horror and what struck, I say, an indelible, perhaps a fatal, mark upon his psyche.

His mother laughed again. Or perhaps there had been only the one solitary laugh which had been suspended, awaiting his ability truly to hear it, for it was inside his head with the acclimatised pitch and colouration of memory. The laugh, that is, had separated itself from his mother. She was with the company downstairs; the sound was here, persistent, and it mocked him.

In such a manner did his own young life submit to the reality of voids and perspectives. The laugh was separate from his mother; the sound mocked him in his darkened room; therefore he was separate (as stars, as lunar flares, as dead matter) from his mother. And this was the greater horror.

Did he not know this before? He had experienced it, but he had not accepted it.

As he was distanced from his mother (so the logic of his feelings now ran) it followed that she was distanced from every one of her family and friends and they from her, and he from them and, likewise and necessarily, they from him, distanced with pitch dark voids between, like stars.

Seemingly fixed, but all moving swiftly in different directions.

He saw then that he must always have known this, and that he had hidden the awful truth from himself out of cowardice, that whenever he had felt himself exposed and vulnerable he had comforted himself with the sense of his family circling him like planets, his mother warming him like a giant and proximate sun, whereas the reality was that they all followed their own individual trajectories, their apparent conjunctions mere tricks of perspective.

'What?'

For again his brain acknowledged the sound some while after the words were spoken. He became aware of a band of light across the floorboards and a draught about his ankles.

'You mean pardon,' said Uncle Mory drawing closer. 'I said that, however fixed they may seem, the stars are, actually, moving away from each other at great speed.'

He spoke this jerkily, in spurts of words between drawn-in breaths, because of his condition. He was an easy man to interrupt but impossible to escape.

'Let's see what you remember.'

Stars, eclipses, gravitation . . . Facts and more facts

were hurled at him, swarming like the firework clusters of meteors which, his uncle informed him, were best to be seen in the night sky in August. The Perseids. When was that? In August. What were these meteors? Shooting stars, debris from space. Good, good, he was learning. Very good.

It was time to pack up the telescope. After all, it was his birthday: they wanted to see something of him before he went to bed. He followed his uncle downstairs with great apprehension.

They were playing bridge. He observed with great clarity how, even as she rose to greet him, crooking one arm in a gesture of embrace ('Darling! We've missed you!') his mother took care to hold the other arm low, turning her wrist so that the cards should be hidden from view. She was partly his mother, partly someone playing cards in a foursome from which he was excluded.

'Tell us what you've been discovering in those vast heavens!'

But although he stumbled through his lesson with an attempt to display enthusiasm, he knew that the answer was unimportant. Her interest was counterfeit. Mentally she had not left her game.

How foreign they suddenly seemed! Was this how the rest of the world saw them – with a cold, dissecting eye?

He watched his mother's sister. If he did not know her as Aunt Hettie, if he were an intruder who happened to stumble into this cluttered room (for the mahogany furniture, the inlaid cabinets with their cut glass, the heavy standard lamps with their tasselled shades, all this forced itself upon him, too, with an aggressive newness) he would think her a petty, tired, unimaginative old woman. That she was, of course. Now he understood the irritation he had habitually felt in her presence, believing it to be his own inadequacy.

'Your turn, I believe, May,' she chided.

His mother scowled in reply. Perhaps it was a mock scowl, for with his mother you were never sure. She was notoriously unpredictable. How magnificent she was! And how wan and tiresome his aunt. Why did she say 'I believe' like that? She knew it was his mother's turn. She wished to seem superior. He allowed himself, for the very first time, the thought that he disliked her.

She wore a wheat-coloured dress which pulled slightly under the arms, and which he also decided he disliked. It came to an end, as she sat, a few inches above a pair of fur-lined slippers. He saw the ribbed impression of her toes on the uppers. He ankle bones stuck out above the fur and seemed ridiculous. He noticed everything.

'Unless we're rushing you,' she added, adjusting her spectacles. They needed no adjusting.

Her husband sat to her left, shirt-sleeved and wearing a tightly-knotted tie, probably regimental. A powerfully-built, red-faced man, he was already a somewhat distant figure, not only because he had been away so long in the recent war but because he held the prime position in the family tableau. ('Make sure to thank your Uncle Jack,' was his mother's constant, desperate admonition.) Even he was altered this evening, curiously diminished.

The arrogant, even bullying, authority with which he presided over them all suddenly brought to mind a large monkey in the zoo with its attendant pack of females and young – self-important but merely amusing to those who looked in from outside. Was he really to be feared? Now he raised his eyebrows in an expression which managed to convey both a criticism and a condescending forgiveness.

'Oh dear,' said his mother, who was partnering Uncle Jack and found herself playing the wrong card altogether.

'Perhaps,' suggested Aunt Hettie, 'we are a little too quick for you, May.'

How could she think so? She could *not* think so. She knew that his mother was finer than any of them. His mother glowed in her separateness, brighter and warmer than Betelgeux, and he wanted to hurl himself across the void like a shooting star.

The fourth player was Aunt Florence, Mory's wife. She never spoke unless speech were absolutely demanded of her. She smiled only if it was expected that she smile. She was utterly correct. He had accepted her as he had accepted them all, but now he wondered why she was so strange. She was strange. She was an oddity. There was something wrong with Aunt Florence. Look how she winced simply to put a card down on the table. See how she held herself tightly in. He knew that it was wrong.

Later, much later, knowing the family story, he was the better able to understand the air his mother gave of being a licensed, wilful child among stern adults. It made his devotion all the fiercer.

She had been born, the last of four children, to a couple too old, too worn for the rigours of parenting. He had been a middle-ranking colonial servant and they had spent their best years under a hot foreign sun, alone. There seemed no reason for their years of childlessness and then, equally, no reason for the sudden arrival of a sprinkling of infants, surprising them like an unseasonal shower.

The first child, a much-beloved boy, a thing of miracle, died in a cholera outbreak before his second birthday. Hettie, then a hard swelling in her mother's belly, was greeted with some disbelief and a great deal of mistrust. They would not allow themselves to accept her permanence, guarding themselves against further grief, and she was brought up largely by the servants, as was common enough in any case. They never learned to find the warmth of her.

It was almost inevitable that Maurice, following a year later, should immediately display all the signs of a sickly constitution. He was nursed, on and off, for years, scarcely surviving the long sea journey home when his father's superiors called him back to England at the end of the Great War. Little Mory was indulged and cossetted, a poor substitute for the deeply-mourned firstborn, but their only son nonetheless. They did what they could for him in the damp and chilly air of the home counties, but remained closest to one another, knowing what could be trusted.

When a fourth baby came along she was in her middle forties and, she had thought, past the possibility of further child-bearing. The couple therefore regarded themselves, though the thought was never expressed, as cheated by life. An innate decency ensured that their new daughter was properly cared for, but they could not bring themselves to respond to her individuality. Servants answered her particular needs. Her vitality, as she grew older, was a weariness to them.

Young May was a damselfly flitting among the colour-less heads of dried-out reeds. She must have felt the frustration early. In her teens, as the vigour of her youth burst from its chrysalis sheath, she must have longed to take dazzling flight. She found friends who, like her, loved to act, to dance, to picnic, to stroll out of an evening under the moon.

Her older sister, prim, meticulous Hettie, regarded her vivacity with disdain. She had already married a man of the same cast as her father, and treated May as a fractious child. Her brother Maurice, the apprentice embalmer, grown bookish and rather precious in the isolations of his illnesses, looked askance at her vitality, which seemed to threaten him. He shrank from knowing her.

She had her child at the age of eighteen and was, even more shockingly, uncertain of its father's identity. Ever resourceful, she had left on a journey to relatives some weeks beforehand, a fictitious journey it transpired, returning with a palpitating little creature in a woollen shawl. Her bright-eyed joyfulness challenged them to throw her out. To their credit, they took her in, and she responded with a gratitude, even a mute subservience, which was ever at odds with her spirited restlessness.

With the death of her parents, both of them gone in the space of a year, she moved in with Hettie and Jack, and was made to feel more beholden still. Her brother and wife lived close by, and she endured the family's stifling embrace with a dull calm which occasionally yielded to a bright feverishness that angered and alarmed them.

None of this did he know on his ninth birthday. Only later would he realise with what detail the knowledge was prefigured in that evening scene at the card table, his mother flickering like a distant star, his uncles and aunts clouding her brilliance, he himself apart, observing as through a sharply focused lens.

The separation, with its stark clarifications, excited him as it frightened him. Each evening would find him excusing himself from the company to sit by his telescope, apparently to learn the motions of the heavens but in reality to sit stiffly on his chair, breath held, straining for sounds from below. He imagined that he could see each one of them distinctly, and a cough, a laugh, the crash of one of the fire dogs against the fender, would act as peremptory stage directions for the latest episode of the play.

Then he would imagine their talk, sometimes creating only the weight and colour of it because the actual content was (as so often in reality) beyond his comprehension. Rigid, eyes closed, he would manipulate his actors – not as a god, with complete control, but according to their given characters, which he now under-stood with a keenness which was at once exhilarating and terrible. This was his guilty secret, about which he fanta-sised through the long hours of the day, yearning for the moment when he could mutter his excuses and hurry up the stairs to the darkened attic room.

His uncle, believing him to be an aspiring astronomer, plied him with books and erudite conversation, and he did begin, haltingly, to learn the rudiments of the science: declination and right ascension; azimuth and the ecliptic; the aurorae and the sidereal day. Strive as he might, however, he could not maintain his hold on the reality of the stars. He knew their reality but began to lose the experience of it. They gradually became emblems once more, mere signifiers. He could not be doing with precession, with parsecs and parallax. It was less a question of intelligence than application. They offered a useless meaning.

This was revealed to him one afternoon as he browsed through a worn and musty book, one of those written at a time when an accomplished, if for today's taste somewhat otiose, literary style was regarded as essential even for a scientist. In a chapter about the death of the stars he came upon this (no doubt ludicrous) sentence: 'We humble time-dwellers inhabit a universe of a hundred thousand scattered bones'. The conceit surprised and thrilled him in a way which the prosaic facts themselves could not, and he returned to it again and again in wonderment and joy.

He knew then that it was the vivifying power of words which was to dominate his life, their elasticity, their plasticity and, above all, their independence; knew that he could never be seduced by pure, arid denotation, but only by the rich, suggestive, fluxive connotations of words.

2 Furnished with Chambers, yet rarely finding poetic voice (6)

I well remember that battered old volume, its red board covers scuffed a honeybrown at the corners where the laminations were revealed. It was the concise edition of the great work, but it sat with a generous heaviness in the hands of young Goethe. He carried it everywhere, and could even be seen, when his attention was apparently elsewhere, to give it a furtive and affectionate pat – rather as quite normal boys will nurse a cardboard box in which lurks an absurdly doted-upon pet spider or a bemused and ravenous stag beetle.

'Bit of a mistake to have played the deuce,' Uncle Jack would reprove his mother at the card table, and (curled tight and apart on the leather sofa) he would hungrily riffle the pages in search of the word, its meaning, its correct pronunciation, its etymology, his eyes then automatically, opportunistically, darting to the words above and below – the lovely, decadent liquidity of *detumescence*, the progression of the soft and the harsh in *deus ex machina*. It was impossible to stop.

Words had become incense to him, at once perfumed, cloying, intoxicating, exotic. Their flavours saturated the mundane world, impregnated gross, unyielding materiality, hung thick and heavy in the air he rapturously breathed. He might suffocate on a honeyed phrase and die happy. He might drown in a richly seasoned polysyllabic stew.

He inhabited a world aswim with words. They bathed

and almost stopped his senses. They were aroma, savour, melody, rhythm. They touched and clung.

How had he come by the dictionary in a house so bare of books? It must have been discovered in his mother's room on one of those occasions when, she having mysteriously disappeared for the evening (an abrupt, energetic wrapping round of arms, a scented kiss carefully applied by glossed lips), he crept from his bed to gaze upon, to touch, to explore, those pathetically few possessions which defiantly proclaimed her individuality.

Her trophies and mementoes were, if the truth be told, commonplace and unremarkable: a lacquered jewellery box littered with cheap brooches and earrings, a few faded and brittle seashells, a vivid scarlet bow which had once adorned a box of chocolates, a vulgar gilt-edged invitation card, photographs of frolicsome outings on which the smiles were for ever maniacally fixed.

They were, however, her own. He gingerly lifted a sheet of tissue paper from a cluster of primroses and violets, inexpertly pressed so that the petals were folded and crumpled, the leaves decayed to a smudge of mottled brown. He took an embroidered handkerchief from its box and held it to his cheek.

But he particularly enjoyed handling the practical items which she used every day. Her hairbrush, for instance, with its smooth, pearly handle and the back inlaid with a colourful garden scene – a young man bent on one knee before a girl in a billowing white dress. He could not say quite why he cared for it so much. Was it the hint of his mother's status in another life which excited him? When he turned the brush over he would find a long and slightly greasy black hair clinging tendril-like to the bristles.

She had only a few books, not enough to fill a shelf, but their very existence was a sufficient statement. They spoke of a world wider than the family, of a different, more expansive way of life. There were novels, romances mostly; a set of colourful travel guides; the Romantic poets in collected form; and a copy of the Bible, presented as a Sunday School prize. And there also, until he laid claim to it, was the dictionary, packed with its priceless treasures.

His obsession was to prove as incurable as it was, one must conjecture, unhealthy. What began with a stray sentence in an old-fashioned book of astronomy came to envelop a life. He felt himself sucked into language as an insect is engulfed by the sticky sweetness of a tree trunk's ooze. It filtered experience, giving it a strange amber glow.

At first there were words in isolation, individual words which haunted him. Sometimes it was the sound alone which he found enticing – he would meet *glaucoma* for the first time, or perhaps *percheron* or *grackle* or *rigadoon*, and he would be pursued by its echo inside his head for hours at a time, sometimes for days. Each had its own colour, its own shape, its own odour, its own personality.

Later he discovered the onomatopoeic qualities of words, and he quickly grew in sophistication so that he appreciated not only the obvious whisper of *susurrus*, the clamour of *babble*, but the abrupt abrasiveness of *rasp*, the sharp deftness of *flick*, the laboured movement of *sluggish*. He could feel the tenor of words whose meaning he did not know.

He passed then from the physics of words to their

chemistry, learning how they reacted with one another, giving off light and heat, generating small explosions. He opened the books in his mother's room and read avidly, almost wildly. He was for a time hypnotised by Keats and almost fainted away, indeed swooned, to hear how in their 'wailful choir the small gnats mourn'. This was before meaning had any importance.

In a pocketbook he wrote down each new discovery, grouping together those which seemed mutually attracted by a magnetism of sound or form. He would create strange, powerful yokings, declaiming them histrionically in the privacy of his room, ashiver, in the throes of an ineffable ecstasy.

May we surmise that the growing intensity of his passion was related, at least in some small way, to the increasing absences of his mother; that he hoped to use the magical power of words to, as it were, cast a spell over his young life, and in particular over the fugitive object of his desire; that he thought, sorcerer-like, to draw a special power from what she had herself first touched and had so carelessly discarded, knitting the flexible strands of language to form a wondrous net which might, if wielded with sufficient skill, lure that beautiful, silvery creature, ensnare her and – oh, heaven! – trawl her in?

'Merciful God!' snarls Goethe, with his customary lack of ceremony. 'Can't we be spared these hypotheses? Where do they lead us?'

How shall we know?

'Fact is, you're temperamentally unsuited to this kind of thing.'

I have attempted to give an honest account. No man can do more. I challenge anyone to find me out in a lie.

'Sins of omission, old buddy. You've left everything out. A good biographer builds slowly.'

And irrelevantly, or so it has always seemed to me. Most of our dealings with the world leave us untouched, after all. I believe in recording the significant moments, the epiphanies.

'Epiphanies, my arse!'

I do deeply regret Goethe's lack of refinement.

'Here's a deal. Give us some action and I'll get off your back pronto. Skip the deep thoughts and interpretations, okay? We'll take the language obsession as read. Talking about it doesn't make it any the less despicable.'

I suspect that he desires frankness rather less than he would have us believe. Interpretations, after all, can be dangerous.

'Or, in your case, cunningly beside the point. Camouflage. Who cares about the heady magic of your mother-tongue? Let's have a story.'

As if there were much of interest to relate.

'Dredge up an incident or two, that's all I ask. Inject a little pace. Get the thing moving!'

By the age of twelve he was, if one must perforce generalise, a bright, sensitive, lonely and neurotic child. Having a temperament dangerously ill-suited to the peculiar rigours of an English boarding school, he was, by the strange logic of his social class, therefore thought to be most in need of them. He was packed off with a single ticket, a battered trunk and an effusion of moist kisses from his mother.

Is is necessary to record the consequent miseries? They were the commonplace tortures of a thousand biographies. He was heartily pummelled by well-spoken bullies; coldly rebuked by masters; ignored by the only boys whose good favour he desired; caned by zealous prefects; forced to shiver on the fringe of rowdy field sports, his raw, inflamed legs stung by icy rain.

Through the long day he warded off these terrors with fantastic imprecations, with silent confabulations of syllables, nonce-words and phrases which, only he knew, possessed a supernatural power. At night, in the cold and echoing dormitory, he shrank beneath his sheet and wept.

If it was natural for him to blame his mother for this suffering and to chastise himself for the disloyalty of the blaming, it was inevitable that the separation should further inflame his love. It flared and it raged and she, to be fair, could not possibly have requited this passion with the ardour it demanded, even had she thought to make the effort.

There was a family holiday the summer of his first, temporary, release. He had scampered about the house and garden on his return, a prisoner on parole. Now the cheerful, fresh-painted dissolution of a small seaside resort intensified his feeling of light-headedness. The salty tang of the air, the damp sand between his toes, were potent symbols of his release. How could he be happier?

At first the disappearances of his mother seemed mere accidents. They would all be strolling along the promenade before lunch (Uncle Jack, blazered, leading the troops forward, Uncle Mory, mouth open, bringing up the rear) when he would notice, with a pang, that she had gone. Too desolate to ask the reason, he would proceed in a heavy silence to the restaurant, throwing desperate glances about him all the time they ate.

The mealtime seemed endless. His uncles and aunts consumed their food in a reverential silence. There was boiled cabbage, which he hated. A waiter whose waggishness had evidently been over-indulged tried to make him laugh.

When all hope was lost and they were sipping their tea, he his lemonade, she would suddenly appear among the detritus of the meal, a meteor-shower in a dark sky, throwing herself into a chair and suggesting brightly how they might enjoy themselves that afternoon.

'Let's have ice creams! Shall we? And a boat trip!'

He burned with pleasure and relief at such moments, his tumid love quite vindicated. When she held his face between her hands, tilted his head and called him her darling, he felt the onset of tears. He felt he might be as precious to her as he needed to be.

By and by, however, the betrayals became too frequent. She would be gone not only for an hour or two, but for a whole day. Her evening appearances were rare and brief. He therefore allowed his feelings less light and air. As the holiday progressed he felt himself in the thrall of a soft sadness. His love for his mother must, for protection, become a secret. Indeed, he half concealed it from himself, so that, when it fleetingly emerged from hiding, it had the poignancy of a sweet memory suddenly recalled.

Most mornings they sat on the beach. It was an unusually fine summer. He wore only a pair of canvas trunks, and the sun roasted his flesh, which first turned an itchy red and then began to peel.

There were rock pools, and he would abandon the rest of the party to explore their frondy recesses, his bare feet slipping on the sea-pounded boulders and their coverings of slimy wrack. Bending low over the water, he felt as alone in this strange world as he had when peering through his telescope. Here the stars were shells, anemones and tiny darting fish.

One day, as he swung an arm dripping with water from the depths of a pool, he met, eye to eye, a girl of about his own age who stood with a yellow plastic bucket in her hand. He was, for the record, grasping the shell of a crab, safely behind the claws in the prescribed manner. His visual memory, however, for ever after registered only his own arm, with the water falling from it in droplets, and, framed by the arch, the face of the girl: blond hair wet from a dip in the sea, salt-encrusted lips, large eyes.

She bent down and scooped water into her bucket. He dropped the crab inside. There was no need for words, and so they said nothing. And then, of course, they laughed at the sheer adroitness of their dumb show. Afterwards there was again to need to speak for some time as they clambered among the rocks, finding limpets, sandhoppers and starfish, he holding out his hand from time to time to steady her.

Her name was Margaret. He called her Marguerite. Nobody had done that before, and she told him so. Then they both liked the name more than ever. They loved hotly and innocently for eleven days. Sometimes their hands would touch under water as they swam, and their fingers would curl and cling, but as if by accident. They would not dare to look at one another in those moments. Or, kneeling to dig in the sand, they would find their thighs inadvertently touching, warm under the sun, and would not hurry to move away.

It is perhaps tempting to see in the youthful Goethe's gauche feverishness a highly-charged transference of that thwarted love for his mother to the first suitable object of desire. I leave that ploy to our growing army of sour reductionists only too happy to deny the spontaneity and generosity of human feeling. And I ask: how explain Marguerite's equal devotion. Was her young life similarly blighted?

Late one afternoon, as they sat fishing in a pool, it occurred to him that, in their dreamy mutual obsession, they might become fused, not separate. The thought was inspired by the sight of their two shadows thrown across the glistening sand, very close. If, he reasoned, he raised himself a little and moved behind her, their two shadows would merge completely. He rose shyly, manoeuvred his body with great precision – and realised, on the instant, that she now had no shadow at all.

He never saw her again.

For days he patrolled the sand with a spreading despair which burned his chest and threatened to burst through its walls. Perhaps her parents had kept their departure date a secret for fear of upsetting her. Perhaps there had been a last-minute change of plans. A persistent projectionist ran and re-ran a series of banal yet intensely move filmscripts in the dark and silent flea-pit of his imagination. He could not believe that she had intentionally left without a farewell.

It was a loss from which he never recovered. The statement perhaps sounds absurd, overblown, but he ever afterwards traced his malaise to this moment. Perhaps, in truth, it marked not the onset of the malaise but his realisation of it.

'Are we philosophising once more?' asks Goethe, with a sidelong glance.

As if reflection were an escape from reality, rather than a means of understanding it.

'As if, indeed.'

But what can be said of Goethe's life in dull, prosaic, concrete terms? Should I tell of his debagging in the quad? Of his winning the French essay prize?

'Why not?'

He made himself inviolable. He discovered that nothing was unbearable once it had been transfigured, idealised by language. He turned to literature and read avidly, drunkenly.

Yes, he was debagged in the quad (one especially frosty December evening); was humiliated on the rugby pitch; was ragged and teased by boys younger than himself. These events passed, however, on the far side of that shimmering gauze of language, which became ever more dense and richly hued, a shuffling of images whose crucial relationships were with one another rather than with a hostile world he might otherwise have experienced in its nakedness, he in his nakedness.

He lived timorously, his friends those who posed no threat to his essential privacy. Quiet types, some of them quaintly studious, they none of them possessed that awkward, probing cast of mind which so unsettled him. He registered these pallid friendships and was glad of them, but what they offered was always filtered through that fluid, filmy substance he spun out of his own head.

I invite you to observe the youth in his seventeenth year. He has, by now, grown very tall and, since he has put on little weight, his body and his limbs appear strangely out of proportion. He nevertheless patrols his world with a kind of confident somnambulism, for he is respected even as he is ridiculed. He is a scholar with a gift for languages. His very narrowness, his dogged devotion to whatever it is that drives him, earns respect for its evident seriousness. He is possessed of a queer gravitas.

What is it that drives him? Books, of every kind. The old dictionary is now so worn, so patched up with gummed paper, that it threatens to disintegrate at every opening. His room is littered with paperback editions, all of which he has read. This is a young man suffering from an obsession.

Yet he cannot write.

There had been a time when he had managed to turn out a few lame verses of an insipid romantic kind: wilting roses, dewy tears, that sort of insufferable adolescent thing. He imagined that the task would grow easier the more he read, but the reverse seemed to be the case. When he read he soared; when he tried to compose he hobbled and crawled.

The truth was that he did not know what he thought or felt. His own inner processes were a mystery to him. Gradually, in time-honoured fashion, he turned his own weakness into a universal philosophy, and he seized upon writing which confirmed him in his barrenness. He came across a poem by Housman:

> *Man has sook the jewel Knowledge*
> *In a casket filled with dross,*
> *Fingers picking at the rubble*
> *To reveal the luminous.*
> *Ah! but on the day he finds it*
> *He will realise his loss.*

He was much taken with the conceit that a loss might be realised just as a profit may be, but he was especially fond of the lines (and learned them by heart) because of their drear epistemological pessimism.

Such a heavy burden of unbelief was sure to take its toll, and charity counsels that we should resist holding up the young Goethe to ridicule for what we may, with hindsight, view as a conventional, a banal *volte face*. Perhaps it was really not quite so simple.

One Sunday evening in October, during a spell of particularly blustery weather, he was persuaded by one of his friends to attend the local Roman Catholic mass. It took him but minutes to regret the decision. The church was cold and stank of incense; the congregation was huddled in a yellowish gloom; although the service was in

Latin, it was recited in such a gabble that he was unable to follow it; and (the President of the Immortals' final sport) the wind blew the candles out.

They were about to pray. He sank gingerly to his knees, seeing nothing, hearing the wind against the panes, the faint creak of wood as the blinded worshippers settled uneasily to right and left along the rail. The priest, used to following his text, was struck dumb.

In that moment of utter peace, that eternal moment, the universe ceased to have delineation, became an indivisible, undifferentiated entity into which he was gratefully subsumed.

Thereafter, taking care not to define the term, he declared himself a believer. He followed a strict regime of prayer and meditation, which served further to set him apart from his fellows.

After his second year at university he made the most profound decision of his life and entered the monastery.

3 Retreat for the wounded – and ruled (3,3,3)

His craving was to have no identity. During those first few weeks within the chilly walls of his voluntary confinement this single thought would not be stilled, but shouted aloud in the silences of his cell, chimed antiphonally with the Latin of the Gregorian chants, wrote itself in rising, heavenward rising, wreaths of cloudy incense: 'Let me be unknown'.

In this, as in much else, he was extreme. Individuality was not greatly prized in that place. The first book he ever read about the order obscured its authorship through the formula 'by a Carthusian', and when he came upon the small monastery graveyard it was to find a random grouping of simple wooden crosses, rough-hewn and unmarked. These things pleased him, but they were not enough. He longed for an impossible total anonymity in the here and now.

Throughout his novitiate he adopted the name Anselmes, partly for its echo of the great abbot, archbishop and saint, but most of all for its anagrammatical significance.

> *'Forgive an obtuse interruption,' begs Goethe, 'but are we to learn nothing of a man's motivation for taking the tonsure? Rather more interesting than all this anonymity stuff, I'd say.'*
>
> *But as it happens, I'm saying. Perhaps the Anselmes business embarrasses him. An obsession with one's own name hardly seems fitting material*

for a monastic mind. It's a poor kind of anagram, in any case, which depends upon the invention of a new word. One wonders how on earth it was supposed to be pronounced.

'The final -es was silent. May I prompt your memory about a certain incident which had some bearing on all this?'

A vague prompt, which I find easy to resist. Goethe did enter a monastery . . .

'And, at length, left it, old cock. I don't suppose we shall learn much of substance about either decision. Plenty of candles, canticles and cowls, no doubt. A thurible or two. Colour, but no depth of field.'

How describe the experience without these things? It was a hermit order, governed by the bells calling the monks from their cells to the services in chapel. They carried candles, they wore cowls . . .

'But how did it feel, *by St Jerome?'*

Ha, Mr Jeer Most! A fitting adjuration, if I may say so.

'Not a jeer, dear heart, but a plea. Come, prey on our hideous voyerism! Withdraw the bolt, lift the latch and let us in.'

Cold, it was always cold. He had a spacious cell on two floors, with a small vegetable garden of his own and a view over the cloister garth where there were fruit trees, plums and apples. There, on rare occasions, he would see one of the monks, hooded, keeping his almost perpetual silence. He was alone for most of the day and night, save when he opened the hatch to take in food from a lay brother in the corridor outside or joined the sandalled queue into the chapel to sing and pray.

It was a life to test the inner strength of any man, but Goethe was surely equal to it. Had he not been locked within himself for years? His cell was bare of luxuries, but the hard bed was as he liked it; he had a large oak desk to work at; there was an oratory for his devotions, and a cold water tap for when his thirst was other than spiritual. Indeed, cider brewed on the premises was available should he have wanted it, but alcohol had always gone swiftly to his head and after the first refusal he insisted that it should never be offered to him again.

He was given a device with a single string for practising the pitch of notes for the chants, but no true musical instruments were allowed for fear of improperly exciting the passions. Goethe, however, had music enough. In the vast stretching silence of the monastery the rich and enticing sounds of words began to well up in his ears, words released from all sequential thought, random, reckless, extravagant, and he struggled with them hour by hour, fighting them away as visitations of the tempter. He felt then that he was going mad, his brain seized by whispering syllables, by orotund phrases which echoed and echoed, by spaghetti strings of senseless incantations which tormented him through the night and were still winding and unwinding as the first light of day touched the grey stones of the wall by his bed.

Distracted, he forced agonised prayers through the minute reticulations of these relentless babblings, for all the world like some whiplashed criminal mouthing a plea for pardon through the latticework grille of the judge's window. If it should be the divine will, he offered, he pleaded, let the power of manipulating words be removed from him for ever.

When the torrent persisted, his supplications apparently unanswered, he devised a desperate therapy, taking a pen and scribbling down as many of the words as he could pluck from the fast-flowing tide of his own mental garrulity. Captured, they seemed far less threatening, like stranded fish which had all but gasped their last, but he was perplexed nevertheless by their swashbuckling autonomy, their ability to thrust themselves upon him without his bidding. He attempted to find links between them, but there were none. They were restless spirits, fiends from hell in search of a suitable host. They stank of brimstone.

And then, all at once, they died away. He awoke one morning, fresh and tranquil, his breathing slow, his senses alert, and gazed at a familiar object on the cell wall for a very long time before it occurred to him to name it crucifix. He rose from the bed and poured himself a glass of water: never had he heard its gushing with such an appreciation of jet and swirl and bubble! Never had he tasted its minerals running separately over his tongue.

He understood that the voices in his head had been the last clamour of the outside world, the acute withdrawal pains of an addiction, and that he was free from a bondage which had oppressed him for many years. As an act of thanksgiving he took what had been his most treasured possession and burned it, a few pages at a time, in the narrow grate of his fire. Did he not, from time to time, catching sight of a strange word as the edges of a page began to curl, leap forward to snatch it from the flames? He had lost that passion entirely. Once the task was completed he took the ashes to the monks' graveyard and scattered them among the crosses, corpses with no names.

The monastery had a fine library, wood-panneled with a gallery reached by a curved staircase. Here he ran his fingers over vellum-bound volumes of canon law, moral and dogmatic theology, Greek and Latin patrology, spirituality, hagiography, modern translations of the fathers of the Church. When he took them back to his cell, signing his name to each for the borrowing period of two years, the words (English, Latin, Greek) no longer sang and danced, no longer had taste and smell, but were docile, humbled, at the service of religious scholarship.

This was his unchanging way of life: solitary meditation and prayer; a scant diet devoid of meat, with but one meal a day at half past eleven in the morning, and this reduced solely to bread and water on Fridays; an assembly in church for the three Hours of Mattins, Lauds and Vespers. He took to his bed at eight in the evening and rose again at midnight for the long Night Office. He returned to his bed at three and left it at first light. He recited the Hours in his cell throughout the day, read extensively, wrote a little, prayed. For the sake of his physical health he would occasionally take a trowel to the weeds of his square of garden. On Saturdays he would join the other monks and novices for an austere and silent supper of soup, eggs or fish and vegetables in the white-washed refectory. On Sunday afternoons, if the weather was fine, they were permitted to take a turn round the monastic farm and even outside the gates and into the nearby village. On these occasions they might talk in a subdued manner. He rarely went.

What was the purpose of his life? To know God, to praise Him and to petition Him for the forgiveness of all mankind. These aims Goethe strove to achieve. He sought God in his meticulous readings, in his assiduous prayers, in his relentless meditations. He offered praise alone in his oratory and with the brothers in the high-vaulted, richly-decorated church, standing before the large, leather-bound antiphonaries with their black Gregorian block-notes. His voice was not rich, but he sang in tune. Prostrate in his cell, he begged mercy for sins committed since the very beginning of the world.

'But is it yourself you pray for?' queried his spiritual guide, with a merry little smile which at once put him on his guard. He had then been at the monastery almost a year and well understood how these meetings combined elements of the tutorial, the confessional and the psychiatrist's couch.

'And should I not, Brother John?' he replied innocently.

'For ourselves last, Anselmes. Then certainly!'

It was a bright afternoon in late spring. A shaft of sunlight danced with dust particles in the chill of Brother John's cell.

'We sometimes will more for our fellow men than we are able to feel, don't you think so?'

Brother John's feet were encased in thick grey socks which dimpled where the stout straps of the sandals squeezed them in. There was a darn at one big toe, in brown wool.

'Is it that I appear to lack humility?' Goethe asked, rushing to fill the silence that was developing between them. He calmed his voice. 'Have I been unkind?'

'No, no. It's more an absence,' Brother John had lived out of time for so long that he felt no compulsion to push his thoughts ahead of their effective expression. 'I am aware that you came to us weighed down by a crippling burden. We have spoken of it before. You know how dangerous such a burden can be, that it can . . . get in the way.'

'I have striven to loosen it, Brother John, with God's help.'

'Indeed.'

Was that affirmation or doubt? Goethe felt a flash of anger, which he instantly controlled. He knew how vulnerable he was to his mentor's criticism.

'Believe me, Brother John, it is less a trouble to me than it was. Something so heavy can't be expected to disappear in a puff of smoke.'

A stupid thing to say. This was no occasion for the colloquial.

'I had hoped,' Brother John continued, thankfully moving in another direction, 'that a more easy view of yourself would lead to a greater warmth for others. I overstate the case, no doubt, but it appears to me that – present company excepted, shall we agree, for the sake of argument and, indeed, of civility – you find tolerance of the human kind barely sustainable. No, of course I overstate the case!'

But it could not now be unstated.

'Love has many meanings,' Goethe protested. '*Agape* . . .'

A thick and hairy hand waved his answer aside: 'No, let's not talk theology at this point. Simple humanity, Anselmes. I speak as your human counsellor now. I've watched you many times with the monks and novices. I've heard what you have told me in this room. There is something not at ease here.'

'There's a rule about liking other people?'

'Pish and tush! Is that the expression?' He smiled and actually patted Goethe lightly on the knee. 'There are several who try my patience, believe me! But to feel so coldly - that is not healthy for one who wishes to live permanently as we do.'

'I have been more recently in the world than you, Brother John.'

'With greater opportunity to practise lovingkindness, Anselmes. I should like to see more of that.'

The hours shrink inside a monastic cell. A passing thought may expand to fill the hours between Nones and Vespers. For days and nights he tussled with his dryness. He made a supreme effort to visualise all the people he had known and to focus on some good thing they had done. He knew that to counterfeit a feeling was futile, but he kept alive the hope that these individuals from his past would, against all the odds, stand warm and – how could it be? – *loveable* before him.

When all these strenuous efforts seemed destined to fail he turned to a more practical expedient. In chapel he attempted small acts of familiarity, his smiles sometimes returned, on other occasions met with expressions of disapprobation, as if he were guilty of an embarrassing solecism. At their communal supers he took care to be first to pass the warmed stainless steel dishes or to pour the water for the brothers to either side of him.

He joined the Sunday afternoon expeditions, too. Up to a dozen of them would plap-plap along the lane to the village, nodding mutely to any locals they encountered, returning by way of a footpath that passed a stables, a couple of farms and a derelict watermill. He had imagined jocular conversations, perhaps some good-natured back-slapping, a vouschafed confidence even, but the monks seemed interested in little more than desultory chit-chat about nothing much in particular. He had no talent for this, and when he tried to inject a personal note he failed miserably. The words would not come.

It was by the header pond of the mill. A grey wagtail was flitting gracefully over the water, and he and Denis, one of the younger monks, had paused to admire it.

'You have a sister,' he said, too weightily he knew. It was meant as a question but emerged as a ponderous statement.

'I *have*?'

'Oh, I thought . . .' Certainly the man had said something about a sister. Had he meant a nun, perhaps? It was nothing, but he could find no lightness, no way of word-skipping away. 'Families . . .' he tried to begin again.

'There's another!' cried Denis, seeing the wagtail's mate join it in a momentary serial dance under a small iron bridge. There were flashes of bright yellow as the sun caught their underparts.

'I was the only one,' he persisted desperately. 'Child, I mean. So neither of us . . .'

Denis gave him a severe sidelong glance as he moved

away, rather hurriedly, to join the rest of the party: 'My sister lives in Australia,' he said with a shrug, 'and I haven't seen her for years.'

He was useless at this kind of thing. Why had Denis seemed to deny that he had a sister? Why was it so strange that someone should have asked? Perhaps it was because his insincerity showed. It was obvious that he didn't care. He really could not care. He had no warmth for Denis, so how could he possibly have any interest in his sister? And what could he do about his lack of warmth for Denis? Where was the kindling? The problem, in various guises, occupied him for days, until he decided that seeking to know God was of far more importance than fumbling with mere human feelings and he returned to the more profound, the potentially far more rewarding, quest.

How shall we characterise Goethe during this period of crisis? If we regard him as driven we court the risk of questioning the work of all religious who apply themselves to arduous duties with a devotion beyond the endurance of the average man or woman.But he was driven. He began to compose a treatise on the nature of God, but never progressed further than twenty pages without destroying everything that he had written. New insights had come to him and he must start afresh. No sooner had he explored these deeper recesses of the problem, however, than yet vaster possibilities would open up to him. He worked at an ever more feverish rate and sometimes left his food untouched for three days at a time.

At last he began to miss the services in chapel. Seduced

by the urgency of his task, he made no attempt to excuse himself through sickness or any other subterfuge, but irritably dismissed the lay brother who had been sent to enquirer into his absence. A session with Brother John chastened him somewhat, and brought him back into line, but his project continued with as much fervour as before, and repeatedly to the same effect.

The end, when it came, was farcical. Like some head-strong public schoolboy who rebels against being gated, he escaped over the wall by night. He was, of course, no prisoner and might have left by the front door in broad daylight. True, the average novitiate would have found that embarrassing, but our knowledge of Goethe's state of mind hardly suggests that such a triviality played any part in his strange behaviour. Was he fleeing in panic from some epic struggle with God Himself?

He bolted by the most direct route, and with a ladder which he found propped against an apple tree in the cloister garth. In his cell they found the umpteenth draft of his seminal work on the nature of God. The first sentence, which was as far as he had got, read: 'He is in hiding and will not come out.'

4 Mood pill can't remedy? Apparently so (3,9)

If the past (to paraphrase a dead poet) already contains the future, was Goethe's very skeleton not visible through his tautened skin during this crisis? Yes, he was a walking cadaver. The game was already up.

See him walking the city streets: he takes deep breaths and yet feels himself drowning; kicks out his legs energetically before him, but softly sinks; turns his head this way and that among the bustling crowds and hears only a fizz and bubble in his ears.

We are the hollow men . . .

The doctors did what they could. Their nostrums slowed his heartbeat and reduced his temperature. God, however, remained hidden.

Perhaps if he had acknowledged the cause of his malaise . . ? He could not. He was truly unable. He only knew that it was what it had always been, and that sometimes he very nearly grasped it. When he turned towards it with an accusing finger, however, it slipped out of view like a fleck of shadow when the sun goes in.

The days became weeks and the weeks months. He scrutinised his face in the glass one morning and saw the passage of years. Time past and time present were a joint reproach: his life was a worthless thing to be regarded with the bitterest odium.

6 Restrict stuff included in crossword puzzles initially (5)

'Nickel odium.'

The words had begun to return. He heard the stupid phrase declare itself inside his head and he shivered. The words of a popular song: 'Put another nickel in – in the nickel . . .' Odeon. He tried to say it, but the other word was stronger. Had he not been spared this torment after all?

He ran the water. 'All I want is laving you.' His mouth split in a mirthless grin, mocking his helplessness against the eruptions of his own volcanic brain. No, it was not funny at all.

Goethe escaped the house and sought the busiest public places. Never again that teeming solitude he had endured in the monastery his mind tortured by hideous, malformed lexical demons. Now he approached complete strangers, buttonholed unwary passers-by, engaged in loud, violent conversations with shop assistants, desperate to drown the inner babble he feared to hear.

There were incidents which later, in rare moments of calm, he was to recall with embarrassment. He was ejected from a theatre where, frightened by the careful silences of a Pinter play, he had offered brusque interpretations of an obscure story-line; spent several hours in a police cell after delivering a lengthy lecture on Thomist theology to a poor housewife whose vacuous nodding he took for encouragement; was pelted with small stones by schoolboys who took objection to a wild-haired, gangly intruder shouting encouragement to them as they went about their playground games.

'A madman, in short?' Goethe demands, rather too jovially for my liking.

No, not quite mad. Disturbed, certainly. But you knew what you were doing, always. It was a matter of self-defence.

'In a life of self-defence, alas. Of perpetual fearful reaction, wouldn't you say?'

What nonsense the man talks! Did you not overcome these terrors by commendable positive action? Bravely striking out upon new ventures . . .

'Brave, my arse,' comes the predictable jaundiced retort.

It took some courage, I should say, to submit himself to the disciplines of the market place, and particularly to its inherent dangers. For he took up translating, accepting small freelance commissions and daring the French and German vocabulary to mingle with the English in dizzying acrobatic neologisms. This would sometimes happen when he was tired and alone, but he found that as long as he concentrated on his labours he was free of the insistent lunatic voices. He was an excellent linguist and applied himself to the work with feelings of relief and gratitude.

Employment was intermittent, but he had no pressing need of money. Uncle Mory had died, gasping his last breath at the very seaside resort where the young Goethe had met and lost his Marguerite, and he had left a bequest of surprising generosity considering his nephew's gradual but undeniable distancing of himself from the family. Goethe never returned home now, and wrote only the curtest of notes to his mother if communication could not be avoided.

He came to compile his first crossword puzzle purely by chance. A fellow translator, who augmented his income by devising a range of brain-teasers for the magazines and newspapers, found himself close to several deadlines just at the time he was given the manual for a German tape recorder to turn into English at extremely short notice. Since he had observed Goethe filling an idle moment by solving a cryptic puzzle at impressive speed, his choice of stand-in was obvious.

'Nothing too abstruse,' he counselled. 'Flatter the reader a little is my motto.'

Those first puzzles were but grey, well-mannered exercises. Later he began to experiment, not only expanding the referential breadth of his creation, but becoming ever more audacious in his verbal and intellectual conceits, in the clotting and tangling of their multifarious subtleties. For the reader he cared nothing; for the wit of the puzzle, everything.

It was, perhaps, another kind of near-madness. There were letters to the editor, and he was obliged to trim his wilder enthusiasms for the public prints. But while subscribers to the *Times* were mollified by a return to more-or-less traditional settings, he continued to intensify the elaborate interweaving of sense and structure in prodigious, kaleidoscopic puzzles which he devised for himself alone.

An obsession? No, more a calling. He had no gift but this private, codified use of words. In society he was gauche. Those few people who claimed to know him a little found him strange, detached. He might speak, earnestly, heavily, rather too loudly, but he was unable to communicate. In these cryptic clues, however, he had found a form of expression which released his knowledge, his philosophy, his humour, his whole cast of mind.

Year by year he perfected the art and science of his métier, in preparation for what was to be the greatest crossword puzzle of his life.

7 *Engage treacherous fellow in wild duel – of the verbal kind (8)*

'Enough!' commands Goethe. 'You've tried and failed, old man. Biography is an art. You haven't got it.'

The cry of the wounded biographer down the ages, I should say.

'No more of this tedious life which drifts listlessly to its turbid close.'

Is he aware of something that has escaped me?'

'Let's introduce a little honesty.'

I hate lies. My loathing of lies is almost pathological. My last lie was told at the age of five years and three months (it was a Tuesday afternoon) and the shame of it is with me still.

'A costive morality, my diddums. I'd be happy with a few squeezed out whoppers in return for the occasional healthy expression of big-T Truth.'

Then perhaps you had better tell the tale yourself.

'Do I have your permission? I thought perhaps the thing was in copyright. But I'd rather tease a few meanings out of your own scribblings first. Where shall we begin?'

I have nothing to add.

'Unwise, I'd say. Sure, *qua* material for textual analysis the document can stand as it is. You're just an embarrassment as far as that goes, awkwardly redundant. Author; text; death of the author - thanks very much, goodbye!'

Isn't this rather callous?

'Completely. Truth tends to be, you know. But I'd keep a close watch on the head-shrinkers if I were you. *Qua* psychological case study your little work is the greatest temptation to professional snoopers since the Wolf Man knocked on Sigmund's door. Just wait till they've been through that confession of yours . . .'

Confession? It's *your* story, dammit, not mine.

'My story, your story . . . What innocence! Everything we write is a confession. Why did we choose this word and not that? Why give precedence to one incident over another? Personally, I'd start with your style. Most revealing.'

Of a decent education, I should hope.

'I was thinking of its tight-buttoned quality. You don't wear a corset, I suppose? Can't stand formality myself. But I'd have most fun with those little stories of yours.'

Stories?

'Oh, the rural idyll, the boxing yarn. Frighteningly transparent, eh? And the young man with the drugs problem. I had to chuckle over that. Once or twice I really thought you were going to kick-start the narrative and hurtle away full-throttle. It's typical of you that you didn't.'

Did I anywhere suggest that these accounts were fictional?

'There you go again! Fiction, non-fiction. Biography, autobiography . . .'

These well-recognised, tried and tested, utterly commonsensical distinctions are to be regarded as having no significance?

'None whatsoever.'

Whether or not a thing really happened?

'Childishly beside the point. But the fact that you

thought it worth writing down - ah, that's another matter. That's where the man stands revealed. And how!'

If this were truly the case a neutral statement would be quite impossible. About anything at all.

'But of course!'

That two and two are four, say. Or that the earth's sidereal period is 365 days, five hours and 48 minutes.

'Plus 46 seconds, if memory serves. Many thanks for the example, professor. Most telling.'

It's an indisputable fact.

'But why should the likes of you and me care about such a pointless figure? Why should it spring to mind as an example? To the knowing we give ourselves away all the time, my dear friend.'

I like to choose my friends, thank you.

'A look, a mannerism, a tone of voice - everything connects. Man's a totality, you know. You certainly are. We've learned so much about you, thanks to your splendid indiscretions. All those revelations, portentous and trivial.'

I deny a single one.

'Especially the trivial. Little girls pursued through fields of cowslips, boxers sweating on the ropes . . .'

What, precisely, am I supposed to have revealed?

'Oh, so much, so very much! And you imagined you were simply protecting the virtue of poor old Goethe, who has every reason for feeling exceedingly miffed. As if that was the worst he could do! Tell you what - let me complete your little stories for you. I'll show you what to make of your pallid fictions. Let's have the unguarded, unexpurgated versions.'

If this is to be a sordid --

'See, you know more than you let on!'

I recognise a treacherous serpent when I meet one. I'm aware that the modern vice is to delight in soiling the unblemished. I know what kind of outpourings to expect from the sump of a diseased mind.

Fiction that's false shan't pay! (8)

Young Seed was by now so far gone in his retreat from reality as to pose a threat to my own well-being. What had begun as a reasonable promise to be of some small service to an old friend had grown to a commitment of great inconvenience which I could not, in all human decency, disavow.

One fine spring morning he rang my bell at an hour which would normally have found me still in bed. As it happened, the bright sunlight had woken me, and I was sipping an orange juice on the verandah. I ushered him inside, making to attempt to disguise my exasperation.

'Don't desert me now!' he began to plead in melodramatic fashion, throwing himself to the floor despite the presence of several well-upholstered chairs.

'Pull yourself together man,' I found myself commanding him. 'And do get up.'

He pushed himself to his knees. 'Can't you see,' he demanded, 'that you represent sanity and order to me? You seem to understand everything.'

'What nonsense!' I replied curtly. 'I am simply in control of my thoughts and emotions. This no doubt seems remarkable to you, since you have no grasp of either.'

'Oh, it's true, it's true,' he began to weep. 'And yet I feel that I'm always so close to it – to discovering the great secret.'

'Secret?' I remembered his disastrous search for spiritual enlightenment with the eastern sect which had, apparently, failed him. 'What are you talking about, man?'

His eyes opened wide, bright with tears.

'Why, the key to the universe and my place in it. Isn't that what we all seek? Don't be angry with me, but it's what you seem to have found already. It's as if there were so many clues to understanding one's relationship with whatever it is that governs our existence, and I can't manage to solve a single one of them.'

I could only shake my head at his gauche juvenile gibberings, which he should surely have outgrown long since.

'There is no key,' I retorted bluntly, 'and therefore no clues which might lead you to find one.'

At this he collapsed on his face, his shoulders heaving.

'Then I'm lost!' he groaned at last. 'I'm nothing but a pointless shred of matter cast adrift in an awful black void . . .'

Rhapsody for ardent follower? State of great agitation by the sound of it! (8)

She led me on through the soft drifts of the yielding feathery grasses, my heart burning fierce as a glowing cinder, and grown to bursting inside my aching ribs.

124

At the stile she paused, and raised a hand as a shield against the brilliance of the sun. The fair had come to the heath, bringing to our ears the hurdy-gurdy swell of the steam organ and the thin, spiteful cracks of the rifle range; dazzling our eyes with the bright, flagrant colours of the Big Wheel and the Whip; assailing our nostrils with mingled smells of candyfloss and engine oil; and challenging our complacent moral composure with the alluring taste of a raffishness quite foreign to our unworldly rural community.

She lifted a foot to the high stile's strut, her flimsy dress sliding up so far as to reveal the place where the thigh meets the first delicious swell of the buttock, and I was mesmerised as a rabbit by a stoat, held fast by the hypnotic power of my own rank lust.

I stood rigid for a moment, in thrall to my importunate manhood, which strained against the constriction of those grey flannel trousers, stickily insistent . . .

Triumphant as you box fancy (8)

So you're half-blinded with your own blood, and there's this ugly brute hammering six shades of shit out of you.

That, I have to admit, is when the training pays off because, hoo-bloody-ray, you start back at him with all the smart tricks I ever taught you, a whirlwind of jabs and feints, and within thirty

seconds the great champion of Africa is stretched
out on the canvas like a passable imitation of the
equator line.

What happens next is that some smart alec who
resents paying out his winnings cuts the guy ropes
and the whole bleeding tent begins to sag. That's
too much for the paying customers, who decide it's
time to join in the fisticuffs themselves, and before
you can say Sugar Ray we're all throwing punches
as one another while the canvas collapses on our
heads.

You and I go down together, half suffocated,
totally overpowered, probably haemorrhaging from
half a dozen cuts apiece, and we're pressed so close
I can feel your heart thumping against my chest. It's
then I hear this little laugh from you, right close to
my ear, and I realise that there's something about
this that you're actually enjoying. There's some
pleasure coming from this physical discomfort . . .

Hay in pants spells Romance! (8)

She stepped from the stile into the further field and
moved trancelike towards the fair. Hot-breathed,
tumescent, I swiftly caught her and ripped . . .

11 Ironic, for instance, that nobody does less to subvert a script than I (12)

Don't shoot the censor, he's doing his best!

'Poor Goethe. He fondly imagined that he would be permitted to scrawl his lurid canards across these innocent pages. Not so, sir. Not while the responsibility rests with me.'

Pssst! Someone give him a nudge, will you? Tell him it's all up.

'Obscenities of the worst kind have been narrowly prevented here.'

School's out, tell him. Lessons are over. The Bash Street Kids are about to have their fun.

'Did he really suppose that, scurrilous suggestions apart, he would add anything significant to what had been written before?'

Makes you laugh, doesn't he? Listen O'Dale: you're not in charge any more. I can tell those little yarns whenever I want. In colourful detail.

'I seem to have prevented you rather successfully.'

Really? Then perhaps I'll show you . . .

'No!'

Or perhaps I shan't. After all, there's another story I'd much rather hear told. But you did tempt me, you know. All those pallid evasions of the truth. All those false clues. My versions wouldn't have claimed strict historical *veritas*, I'll grant you, but they'd have probed the recesses of your secret heart, all right. A painful business, eh?

'Heaven forfend that we should ever live in a world

without deep secrets.'

Give me time, Duggie baby. I'm working on it.

'For our dignity . . .'

Which is another of your deceitful evasions. Let's draw back all the curtains! Let's fling open the windows! We'll feel far healthier, you know.

'Speak for yourself.'

Oh, I'll speak for both of us if necessary. I'm going to enjoy myself. But it does seem a shame for you to chicken out at this stage. After all, it was you who started the whole thing off.

'I began, if I may remind you, a technical treatise on the crossword puzzle.'

A terrible mistake, as I might have told you at the time.

'Why didn't you?'

And ruin the sport? I knew I'd eventually manage to put my oar in, if you'll forgive an insensitive expression. You need me, you know. You may despise me, but I'm the guy with the balls.

'That, if may have occurred to you, is precisely why I *don't* need you.'

Sorry if I snigger. But I do respect you, O'Dale. Yes, really! I know my own limitations. No matter the priggishness, you are a decent old stick. You actually try to behave in an honourable fashion. And you're the wordsmith, for God's sake. Why don't we handle this thing together?'

'*Which* thing, precisely?'

As if he can't guess! The story of that magical night, natch. The stars in the velvet sky. The frolics by the pool. Between us we'll remember everything.

'That was long ago.'

And in another country, sure. Back in good old Blighty. And besides . . .'

'Please, no!'

We can't stop now, Douglas. Can't you feel the momentum? We have to tell.

'To what end?'

To the bitter end, I'm afraid.

'But you're not afraid at all. You're relishing this.'

What a swine I am! Here's a reason for you, then – sheer curiosity. Why does a successful undergraduate throw up his studies and enter a monastery? Not quite an everyday occurrence.

'From religious conviction. To seek . . .'

Won't do, old cock. Partial truths are out now. We're playing by the Goethe rules.

'To reassess . . .'

And farewell to abstractions! It's the genuine experience we're after. Come, you can do it!

'If my memory should falter?'

What you forget, I shall recall. And vice versa, no doubt. We're all fallible, Douglas. Who knows better than you?

'It was in the summer of 1958.'

A sound start. It was a Saturday evening in August, if I may prompt you a little. The weather was brilliant. It was a large house, late Victorian, set in a few acres of garden with a hint of wilderness beyond. We'd gone with friends?

'With friends of friends, I believe. We knew practically nobody.'

That's right. We savoured the delicious freedom of the outsider. The feckless hours sped by.

'The sun went down in a ruby haze.'

A great opening, Duggie baby! Let's use it. You're into the spirit of this thing already.

'I make no promises.'

Don't worry, I'll keep you up to the mark. Let's recall your state of mind now. A bit troubled, yes? Well, more than a bit. You're twenty, a zealous scholar, a loner, a searcher after truth . . .

'Don't exaggerate this, please. Everyone has problems.'

Yeah, yeah, so you're an ordinary questing young man who just happens to have jangling nerves, a troubled intellect and some kind of existential problem. That's what they'd have said at the time, wouldn't they? No, don't argue. That's what *I'm* saying, and I'm in charge. Okay?

15 Garbled little account enthralls us. It is abnormally preoccupied with matters of conscience (9)

The sun went down in a ruby haze. The trees were ink-black silhouettes before it, three tall, lopsided pines over-topping a fringe of ornamental maples at the garden's western perimeter.

'And I took a great swipe at the thing,' the beefy young man with the white fluorescent socks was saying. The socks were beginning to glow in the dusk.

'Don't bother to tell me, Jack. I was there, remember. I witnessed your disgrace.'

There were four of them, five with himself, standing by a metal sculpture of a horseman on the lawn nearest the house. Fuzzily indistinct figures were in wavy, dream-like motion all around them, shadows that talked very loudly and laughed and raised glasses to their ghostly lips, the men in shirtsleeves, the women wearing light cotton dresses which lifted at the lightest breeze.

'Just 364 runs short of Sobers' record! The ball took an outside edge, nearly removed third slip's head and was caught by some wretched artisan three inches inside the boundary.'

A match had evidently been played in the village that every afternoon. They snorted and brayed about it for minutes on end, the four of them. He watched the pantomime of their thrown-back heads, their open mouths, their exposed teeth. It was, without doubt, the most hilarious event in the annals of cricket. They slapped one another on the back, on the upper arm, even (with the back of the hand) across the chest.

Slap for pals. Laps for gals. Gals' alps

'And you, old chap?'

Having himself never slapped anyone in his life ever, not in the abandon of horse-play or with anger's intensity (a kind of chiasmus), he being disabled from such shows

'Douglas, is it? Do you play?'

Sad lapse

'Oh, not for many years.'

They ignored him then, this uncommunicative outsider. He followed them for a while, across the lawn to a shrubbery where someone had draped tasteless coloured lights among the bush roses and the hydrangeas, thence to a small marquee where there were ricketty tables heavy with bottles. He dipped his head below the striped awning and joined them inside. It stank of wet grass and light ale. They made great play of slurping beer clumsily into their glasses so that it spilled on their shoes and trousers, and then they went outside again. He took the nearest bottle and poured himself what turned out to be cider.

Disabled, moreover, from something other than mere show, something other than the tedious triviality of flesh upon perishable flesh, that time-borne contiguity

'Been weighing up the opposition, Jack?'

'If you're referring to what I think you are.'

'Don't get touchy, now.'

'I'll give you touchy, for Christ's sake, Frankie. What do I care who she brings?'

'Tra-la-la!'

'Damn you!'

Which is therefore unworthy of our perfervid moralities

When he emerged from the tent they had gone. He was not sorry, yet something disturbed him. It was his own incorporeality. He had seemed to disappear before their eyes as completely as he habitually shrank before his own self-scrutiny. Yet they existed for him, unremarkable though they were: four self-satisfied young men with little to trouble their shallow minds. How was this? He had known them for perhaps half an hour, yet he could name them, describe them, even cite their principal individual characteristics. They existed, whereas he had been forgotten already.

Somewhere, far down a slope, a band was playing. Thin, scratchy sounds reached his ears. The air was still very warm, and small flying creatures seemed to swim through its moistured heaviness, blundering into flower stalks and coming to rest gratefully on bare arms and shoulders. A cloud of gnats dutifully formed a wailful choir and mourned about his head. One dropped to his hand. He saw how carefully it balanced on the delicate filaments of its legs, he watched the dark body engorge.

'Douglas! You can't be alone at a party, not possibly.'

'Mrs Harbin,' he said politely. 'Mr Harbin.'

'No, no, Violet and Herbert,' admonished Herbert Harbin, putting an arm round his shoulder and then quickly withdrawing it. 'And what are you doing with your jacket on in this heat?'

It was true. He was still wearing his dogtooth sports jacket with the white shirt open across its lapels. He was more comfortable that way, but now felt himself obliged to take it off.

'You're an old stick-in-the-mud, Douglas,' Violet Harbin teased, shaking her auburn bee-hive as she looked up at him. She was rather on the short side, but her advantage of perhaps ten years gave her an easy authority he could never hope to possess. Not ever. 'We'll have to take you in hand.'

The Harbins had brought him to the party, and had talked property prices all the way. (He was an estate agent.) They were an unnaturally hearty and eager-to-please couple, connected in some way he had forgotten with the family of a university acquaintance now spending a year in Hamburg. He could not recall either why they were here or how they had come to include him in the invitation. Perhaps he was a substitute for the student of German.

A shooting star swooped through the dark heavens and disintegrated. *Universe of a hundred thousand scattered bones*

'So are you enjoying yourself?' Violet Harbin asked, scampering before them along a gravel path which ran beside a croquet lawn. A few of the younger guests were playing on, despite the fact that the balls had lost their colour – or perhaps because of it. 'Come and meet the Mailers,' she urged, without waiting for an answer.

He met the Mailers. He met the Millays. He met the Fromes. He met the Dunts. He met the Seeds.

Bare, bleached bones, each held, withheld, ineluctably in cosmic separateness, no matter that deceitful, that fantastical time-borne contiguity. No matter

'Come, Mr O'Dale! You're a young man. You can explain these mysteries to us.'

A bright light was shining. That was because they were not far from the house, which had a lamp on one wall to illuminate this corner with its heavy plastic chairs scattered about the grass within the confines of a well-trimmed privet hedge. The leaves gave off an oxymoronic sharply sweet smell.

'Or perhaps you don't appreciate music?' Jimmy Dunt persisted, thrusting his liverish cheeks closer. He had a wheeziness of breath which reminded him of his uncle. He was a meat wholesaler.

'Motets?' he murmured, not knowing what was expected of him. A squall of laughter. He was sitting on one of the plastic chairs and was aware of a pain half way up his back. The cider in his glass tasted sweet, and he was surprised to discover that most of it had gone.

'That hardly qualifies you to judge skiffle,' warbled Molly Frome, whose floral dress (predominantly blue, with a motif of what looked like overblown petunias) was a rebuke to dull Nature.

He knew nothing about skiffle, of course. Was that perhaps the sound he had heard as he left the drinks marquee? Yes, he approved of the neologism. He wondered what instruments they were playing. There was a commendable, appropriate swiftness about the word, an echo of ripple, and the lightness of – well, of a skiff on the surface of the water. And inconsequentiality, too. Piffle.

I'll tell you what I think,' smiled Helen Seed, putting a hand to each side of her round librarian's glasses and tilting forward as if to examine a manuscript. 'I don't believe that Mr O'Dale is a young man at all. Not deep down inside.'

Where the tides do not reach

'Are you, Mr O'Dale?'

'Oh, don't be unkind, Helen,' Violet Harbin came to the rescue in jolly fashion. 'Ignore her, Douglas. Douglas has a mind.'

'But I didn't mean it unkindly. Youth is something we're beginning to have rather too much of.'

'Too bloody right,' Dunt broke in. 'That's what I was saying. The music's only part of it, if you can call it music. Look at the clothes.'

Archie Mailer gave a laugh that was supposed to indicate derision: 'There's some here I wouldn't expect to see. Not if they want to get invited back again.'

'Bootlace ties,' Dunt offered.

'Drape jackets.'

'And what about the violence?' demanded Ron Millay, a mild little fellow who presumably felt the water had warmed up sufficiently for a dip. 'Have you read?'

'Ripping up cinemas. Terrible,' his wife supported him.

'Fighting.'

Someone had refilled his glass. He rarely drank, had never had more than one glass of anything before. He wondered whether it was the cider or the lamp on the wall or something else altogether which gave everything an unaccustomed brightness. His eyes burned.

'As for the morality,' remarked Enid Millay, screwing up her face and evidently having no intention of completing a sentence.

'Quite.'

'It's the American influence,' Dunt stated comfortably. 'They lead and we follow.'

'No respect any more. Not from the young.'

'No example. Take that Jerry Whateverhecallshimself.'

'Lee Lewis. Disgusting. Marries a girl of thirteen.'

Not wishing to deny these remorseless imperatives, these humdrum pieties, fierce and comforting at once, knowing how they sustain us through the squalid commerce of living; but though knowing that, experiencing that as God knows all men must, yet loathing their dull tyranny, craving their supersession

'And got the nerve to bring her here!'

The discomfort was too great. He stood, pushing the instrument of his torture aside, staring at the unbelievable emptiness of his glass. He had not been aware of drinking.

'There,' cried Violet Harbin, 'we've said too much for Douglas! Don't think for a moment that we were criticising you, Douglas dear. It's just the minority.'

'No,' he said. 'Drink.'

'A bloody large minority,' growled Dunt.

'I'm with you, Douglas,' boomed Harbin, leaping to his feet. 'Top-ups all round. We'll get them in. What was it, Enid? Helen? Someone write it down.'

They strolled towards the marquee, Harbin doing elaborate mental sums to estimate the value of the house, garden and adjoining out-buildings.

'If Wymberley ever sells, it'll be my board at the end of the drive. He's as good as promised.'

'You trust him?'

The question surprised them both.

'That's a hell of a thing to ask in the circumstances,' Harbin protested with a short laugh. 'In the man's own back yard, so to speak. When you're enjoying his hospitality.'

'I'm sorry,' he said, utterly confused. 'I know nothing about him.'

'I'll introduce you.'

Harbin found two small trays lying in the grass just inside the tent. Fishing the list from his pocket, and still talking property, he began to fill the glasses.

'Believe me, Douglas, it's the business to be in. Ever thought of it yourself?'

'No.'

'You should. A bright young man like you would go a long way. Now, lemonade in that one, lager here, Babycham in the other, then we're done. I'll be on my way with this little lot. See you in a mo.'

After Harbin had gone he poured the drinks and carried the tray carefully to the entrance. He stood still for a moment, hearing the faint music, seeing the coloured lights in the distant parts of the garden, watching the constant shadowy movements among the shrubs and trees.

Craving

Somewhere quite close at hand a cockerel crew, violently aggressively, ridiculously. With all that noise and artificial light the poor creature must have become painfully disorientated. It was not yet midnight, but that rasping cry rent the air as if dawn were already up. It was a cry to end all darkness.

Within his own breast, he could not describe it otherwise, there came an immediate answering cry. He turned, dropped the tray on a table, and stumbled outside.

∗

'If that's not a giraffe,' a girl's voice saying.

'Shoosh, Carrie!' saying another one

'I'll eat my hat.'

Echoing.

'With only two legs?' Laughing, laughing.

'Others tucked in his trousers. They're big enough.'

'Things you say.'

Echoing off water. Sloshing sounds of.

Craving what can perhaps never be vouschafed, what God cannot allow maybe, can that be true, since it would overthrow that very mundanity which keeps us rooted in what we need to be forgiven for, so needing in turn His grace

'Watch that tall tree now. He'll be feeding, you see.'

Laughing. Blue water, light gleams. Shadows rocking.

'Excuse me, mate. Let the dog see the rabbit.'

'Giraffe, Billy.'

'Eh? I mean the springboard.'

'Never mind,' Laughing. 'Go on, Mr Universe. Double somersault.'

'I might just, then you'll get splashed.'

'Dare you.'

'I might just.'

But no, for if so why gave us this capacity for reaching beyond, for almost grasping, unless of course maliciously, for sport, which cannot be believed

Crashing the water. Squealing the girls. Squeals of seals, real eels their meals.

'Now you've done it, Billy. Now you've really done it.'

'Says who?'

'Says us. Which bits yours, Sal?'

'Ooh, well.'

'First come, first served, I say.'

'Have mercy on a bloke.'

'You that side, Carrie. No escape.'

'Mercy.'

Crashing, and another. Gleams and shadows.

Granting this consciousness, therefore, why unless maliciously not vouschafe more than mere conscience, this tawdry thing time-borne

'And again.'

'One more time.'

'Let him go.'

'That'll teach him.'

'Exhausted. You.'

'Shall we again?'

'No, exhausted.'

'Learnt your lesson?'

For if man not yet ready because not yet redeemed, why torment with visions of what might be, why not subdue to knowledge of duties only, not these visions

Water stilling.

'Enjoy that, Billy?'

'For starters.'

'Saucy imp.Who's next, Sal?'

Laughing. 'Don't you dare, you wouldn't.' 'Wouldn't I?' Closer. 'Wouldn't I?'

'You, Carrie.'

Carrie. Carry. Miss Carrie.

'If I can just squeeze past.'

Visions

'Do excuse me. So slippery here.'

Miscarry.

'Oops, so sorry if.'

Free falling. Tree felling. Cold clutch at chest.

'God, Carrie. What you did.'

Down, out of man's element, head back, limbs stretched, eyes shut, a noise without meaning in the ears, a sudden lack of weight *Where the tides do not reach* a wondrous lack of weight that yields the body up like a propitiation, slack, abandoned, unresisting, a soft release, a reprieve, asway like something casual in the ocean, a coil of wrack, a wreck of wrack, to have no reck but rack and ruin and run *Where the tides*

*

'And did the mermaids sing to you, Douglas,' the American girl asked with a grin.

Anna, that was her name. He had been brought to the house to dry off, and now he sat in a large and stuffy room with mock Tudor wainscoting and pompous padded chairs, another man's clothes on his body. The trousers had a rather loud read and blue check pattern and, though they fitted well enough around the waist, were inches short in the leg.

'I did not linger, Anna, in the chambers of the sea.'

They were both pleased to share the allusions. Should he have added that his trousers were neither of white flannel nor rolled at the bottoms?

When he had first entered the room he thought it peopled entirely by the elderly infirm, taking refuge from the lingering heat of the day, from the torments of the garden with its humming insects and rudimentary seating. Then he had spotted this slim, brown-skinned girl standing by what seemed to be an original Francis Bacon oil painting: he had never seen the real thing before. She had waved in his direction and he had started forward, only to collide with the actual target of her gesture, the skeletal young man of about their own age who now sat at a small table with them.

'Don't understand,' he said, puckering his brow.

'Robin's a mathematician,' she excused him. 'Brilliant, of course, but wouldn't recognised T.S. Eliot unless he had a square on his hypotenuse. There's a lot of under-water business in Eliot, Robin. Poor old Prufrock, Burbank with his Baedeker, Phlebas the Phoenician.

'Why?'

She shrugged: 'A mathematician's kind of question. You think there's a two-plus-two answer? Anyway, you don't want to hear my thesis. Wait until someone publishes it.'

'It's because,' he tried to explain, 'of what it represents. Something . . . liberating.'

'Ha! That's what you felt when you nose-dived into the deep end, eh?' Robin chortled dismissively. 'How positively liberating!'

He could not speak. The tale was already well told, of a clumsy non-swimmer who somehow fell into the pool and was rescued, arms thrashing in terror, looking most comical no doubt, by young Billy Myers. Let that suffice.

'You're an Eliot reader, Douglas?'

'An occasional one,' he told her, the vigorous nodding

of his head betraying more enthusiasm than he meant to convey. He was familiar with most of the poems, had seen a couple of the plays, but he hesitated to claim close acquaintance when talking to a serious student of the canon who was half way towards a doctorate.

She wore tiny green earrings, shaped like serpents. They matched her light shoulderless dress, at which he did not look.

'He's actually a tiresome old fart,' she said, reaching for a plate of prawn sandwiches which seemed to have arrived from nowhere.

A tiresome old fart. He could not believe this. Our farter which art.

'He's still around?' Robin asked with the air of someone who scarcely wanted to know.'

'Sure.' She chewed her sandwich. 'If only just. But he pulled the curtains on life long ago. I think I'll savage him a little.'

He sat forward, strangely agitated, as if a tide broke somewhere inside him and foamed: 'He is, surely, our greatest living poet?'

'Arguably.'

'Is there any argument? In his diction, for instance. A new language for the twentieth century.'

'Okay.'

'And his referential breadth. Hasn't he enriched —'

She waved a hand at him, half conceding, half protesting: 'You can have all those things, Douglas. I'm with you, naturally. Some wonderful lines. It's the sour littleness of the man I don't find easy to stomach.'

'Littleness!'

143

Her hair was nutbrown, glossy and cut short, with a slight wave at the front.

'I met him once. It was a couple of years ago, back home. Shall I tell you? He'd come to give a lecture to the English faculty, and we'd been looking forward to that day like five-year-olds wait for Christmas. We worshipped him, I suppose. It was all a bit unreal. The hall was full to bursting, and ominously hushed, and in he came, right on time – tall figure, somewhat polished and fragile, like an ornament you prize but don't display too often for fear of breaking. He read from a script, as we really should have expected. Subtle criticism in an accent which was still ours, to some extent, but thinned out, you know? Refined.

'Afterwards a few of us were privileged to be introduced to the great man in the principal's study. I guess I've never been exactly shy, so I made sure that I trapped him in a corner for a few minutes. It's not every day you can make small-talk with a literary legend, after all. Ha! That was the first mistake – small-talk he hasn't got!

'Anyhow, we struggled along well enough, with a little about literature and a little about college, and then he thought fit, maybe as a way of moving on to someone else, which I wouldn't blame him for, to give me some worldly wisdom to chew on. I certainly didn't ask for it, but I suppose I had been boring him with some of my possible plans for the future, being an incurable optimist. He fixed me with those glossy reptilian eyes. "Whatever you become," he murmured, "devalue it." That was all.'

'A bald statement. It might be interpreted in several ways.'

'I can't forgive him, Douglas, whatever you may think to plead in his defence.'

'Shall I try?'

'But it's of a piece, don't you see,' (now she thrust her body forward, too, in answer to his own assertiveness) 'with what we find throughout the works. Everywhere.'

'A philosophical strain.'

'A valetudinarian strain. A copping out.'

Their companion, an exasperated expression on his face, stood up and began to stroll away: 'Forgive me if I seek some fresh air,' he said with the weakest of smiles.

'Poor Robin,' she commiserated. 'I do believe he came into the house in order to escape me for a while. He *said* he was looking for the john. He's my devoted English cousin, but he finds my native enthusiasms hard to take. That's because of his own damnable native reserve.'

'Which Americans never have?'

She laughed: 'I take your point, but Eliot's reticence has nothing much to do with the manner he imbued in the nursery. It's a produce of what we might kindly call a rather low temperature. Don't you see that?'

Her eyes were grey-green, he noticed.

'Submit, Douglas!'

'It seems to me,' he said cautiously, 'that he's the poet of infinite regret.'

'Ah, but regret for what?'

'For the loss of civilisation, for instance.I mean, for some grander, some more gracious way of living. The rose-garden, yes? Something lost.'

'Or something never found, maybe?'

He felt suddenly very hot, as if all the windows of the house had been closed and had trapped more clammy air than the fabric could withstand. When he looked abut him he saw, of course, that nothing had changed at all. The room chattered with a dozen conversations like their own.

'What kind of thing may he never have found?'

She leaned back in her chair, another sandwich in her hand: 'Must stop eating these terrible fatteners,' she laughed.

What kind of thing? What kind of thing?

Craving

'Literary people deal with these matters very circumspectly, don't they? Look at Eliot's early life – all that heavy Protestant angst, all that nay-saying. It cut out the light and stopped something growing. Then he became frightened of it.'

'He's the poet of solitude,' he blurted, trying to start again. 'That's what he feared most, perhaps.'

'Oh, yes, a kind of solitude. You can see him making great efforts to overcome it. Marriage didn't work – not his first one, anyway. I don't suppose he had much to give it. Macavity's not there!'

'But honest.' His chest felt constricted and his voice had a strangled sound to it. 'He's always honest.'

'You think so? Well, I suppose he never deliberately lies, of course not. But it's what he won't face up to. He never quite puts his finger on the thing. Did you know he got quite taken with boxing at one time? Really! I don't mean he stripped down for action, lawdy no, but even the thought of him sitting at the ringside give me goose-pimples. Can't see him yelling for blood, can you? What one earth was he up to, would you say? What was the motive?'

'Perhaps there doesn't have to be one.'

'Sure, there always is. Especially when it's so dramatically out of character. Come on, Douglas! Virtuous Gladstone and his fallen women. The muscular thug with Mom tattooed on his arm. The nice middle-class kid obsessed with horror comics. What were fisticuffs doing for Eliot?'

What were fisticuffs doing for Eliot? *Having himself never slapped* He could not breathe.

'One thing's for sure, he couldn't have told us himself. Or wouldn't.'

In the room the ancients come and go, talking of Francis B. & Co.

HURRY UP PLEASE ITS TIME

'Douglas, old man! Where in God's name did you get to?'

Herbert Harbin clamped a powerful hand on his shoulder and swung him round to confront a double row of gleaming pearl-white teeth.

A fat and exceedingly long cigar was pushed into his hand. It felt rough to his fingers, and surprisingly light. He had never smoked one before, and he stared at it for some time, wondering which end was designed for his mouth.

'Wrong way!' barked Dalton Wymberley with a

spluttered chuckle, seizing it, inverting it, thrusting it between his lips and raising a silver lighter to its tip. The flame sprang yellow. '*Thought* I'd seen those trousers before.'

'I do hope —'

'Heavens, no. I'd never get into them these days.' He patted his stomach with pride. 'Successful living.'

'Douglas is at Oxford,' Herbert Harbin said.

'Get down for Christ's sake,' Wymberley commanded.

'I beg --'

'Damn stupid puppy,' he growled, grabbing the collar of a spindly-legged Airedale which seemed intent on bowling over everyone in sight. 'My wife's choice. I need some time at home to train it up.'

Wymberley, circulating, had arrived at the plastic chairs, wherein still sat, still doggedly sat, the Harbins and the Dunts, the Millays and the Seeds, the Fromes and the Mailers.

'Everybody happy?' he boomed in a fruity man-of-the-world manner, waving his own cigar in the air as if it were a banner proclaiming something.

Everybody was happy.

'Must press on. Down, Tarquin! Wonderful to see you all.'

What kind of man was Wymberley? A politician, Harbin had told him, of the Conservative persuasion. A self-made businessman and Member of Parliament. Generous, as witness this lavish annual thrash, opening his house and grounds to every single villager without exception and (how did one put it?) to select worthy members of his constituency. To the horripilant Harbins,

148

for example,To the fringent Fromes, the sebacious Seeds, the desipient Dunts. The kind of man who would offer a cigar to someone for no other reason than that he happened to be wearing a pair of his trousers.

'Managing, old man?' queried Harbin.

You had to suck vigorously to keep the thing burning, and this naturally irritated the throat. The smoke, which had a pleasant tangy aroma, likewise affected the membranes of the nasal passages.

'If you don't mind me pointing this out, you're not supposed to inhale.'

Yet he rather enjoyed attempting to master the art. After the initial coughing and choking he discovered how to coax that terminal glow with more gentle, less frequent, inspirations; learned how to blow softly so that a cloud formed about his head and the rich vegetative pong lingered in his nostrils. The glorious stench almost overwhelmed him. In this, he suddenly understood, lay the hitherto mysterious appeal of cigar-smoking, that cocooned within this flimsy veil one luxuriated in an intense privacy, trembling to the pungent ministrations of the most primitive of our senses.

'Where in Erse did you vanquish, Douglas?' he seemed faintly to hear Violet Harbin ask.

But this or such was Bleistein's way . . .

'He was on the horse, my pressures.'

'Wooing Dot, may one enchoir?'

'Enraged in conservation with a ghoul.'

'A dire curse, eh?'

A lustreless protrusive eye stares from the protozoic slime.

'Calm, Douglas, spoil the bones.'

Universe of a hundred thousand
'Woe is she?'
'Yea, woe!'
'Make a fool confusion.'
A saggy bending of the knees.
'Silvia.'
'Sylvan?'
'That all our swains commend her.'
'Ha! A jerk!'
'He's not being Sirius.'
Smoked like a kipper, he thought. It seemed to penetrate his every pore. He imagined his body juices stained with the stuff. He felt possessed by it.
'But as I was slaying, Jimmy.'
'Unclear disorientment.'
'Burn the bum.'
'That's E.N.D. Disgutting.'
'Sucker for the enema.'
'Bloody rushings.'
The rats are underneath the piles.
'Joust, what thereafter.'
'Your gun to spike your foughts young moan?'
'Oh, I thoroughly deplore the dropping of aitches in any circumstances.'
'You erred.'
'Another jerk.'
'Won't be cirrus.'
'Cant.'
'Young degeneration.'
'Give him the cod soldier.'
Perhaps, he mused, he would become an inveterate

slave to the weed, his fingers burned brown with the years, his cranium forever wreathed in a wispy garland, an odiferous nimbus. Who were the great cigar-smokers of history? Surely they were the most ruminative, the most contented of men!

'Goodness! Lurk what tinnitus.'

The smoky candle end of time declines.

'Mourning.'

'One o'cock. Betelgeux, my sweat.'

'Betelgeux. Ruddy, Douglas?'

'No. Leave me here. Please.'

'Leaf? Are you Ceres?'

'Please.'

'Weak aunt.'

'Please.'

'Howl you --'

'Please, for God's sake, will you please climb into your bloody Sunbeam Talbot with its cramped little back seat which threatens your unfortunate passengers with agonising muscular contractions beyond the febrile imaginings of a Torquemada; will you please shut those beautifully polished doors without even thinking to begin another excruciating conversation about the price of this house and its grounds; and will you, *please* will you, I absolutely beg of your, stand not upon the order of your going but drive away from here at breakneck speed and by the shortest possible route, please!'

'Ah, you quote Will, Douglas?'

He turned his back on them then, moved suddenly by some impulse other than loathing, tossing the butt of his cigar behind him (did he only imagine that it landed in

Jimmy Dunt's scotch, spitting and hissing like a vicious cat?) and careering into a remoter part of the garden, safely dark behind bushes, under trees, where he could sink to his knees unseen.

This or such was Bleistein's way, a convulsive shudder of the loins and shoulders, with the head thrust out – tomato, marmite, pea and cheese.

He retched violently and copiously, a protozoic slime, and again with such force that his breath was lost and his muscles griped, and again and again until every last gobbet of the undigested stew had welled and surged and hurtled, tearing at his throat and depositing a sordid assorted debris in its wake, a mulch of clammy shreds in the interstices of teeth and gums.

All poison spent, he rolled upon the grass and, supine, fell asleep.

He lay, gently wafted, on the bed of a tranquil ocean. When he opened his eyes he remained in those depths, though knowing that what he saw was not the skim of shadow on the surface of the water far above or the refracted glow of a vivid sun, but the full moon bright in the night heavens and the flecks of thin cloud which passed high up across the studded stars. Chiasmus.

Deep in these waters he had no determined rescuer to kick and thrash against, but submitted sweetly to the bob and sway, his torso slack, abandoned, unresisting.

Those are pearls that were his eyes

Some subtle stealing process of dismemberment began

152

to ease and lighten him. He felt it pick him clean down to the bone, soft stripping all the while he gladly yielded.

That sudden dart and flutter was in truth no shoal of little fishes, but an owl that left the shelter of its treetop. Its mate called from a perch nearby: *ke-wick*. He heard it.

I should have been a pair of ragged claws

The water slopped and laved. The flesh had gone, the eyes were pearls, the bones were becoming coral. Becoming coral *Where the tides do not reach* most becoming coral. A mermaids choral.

Sea-girls wreathed with seaweed red and brown

And then the agitations of the brain. O let the lambent waters wash here, too! He lay quite still and the sky was liquid round him.

Shantih

O let these waters . . . He offered every last thing to this ocean. Thelassa thing *God, no* he prayed, *tear off these grotesque fronds which wave* He willed to be unwilled, to have the thickened carapace dissolve, the softer inner parts exposed, ripe for devouring.

Winnowing, winnowing. *Shantih*. He felt the clinging things so firmly clamped upon his mind begin at length to lose their hold. Tugged and teased, they broke off one by one and slowly lifted, drifting.

The space above was very clear and still.

Chaos of words was gone, first gone, those ugly writhings gone; and now the outer husk of thought began to crack and crumble, the time-worn phrases, notions turned to fossil. They broke away. He let them go.

Shantih

He let them go.

153

The unchecked waters scoured, abraded. They tore at overhanging things, they undermined the porous rock. Time flooded.

He passed the stages of his age and youth

At length he saw emerge a shape resistant to erosion, a shape at once familiar and yet unutterably strange. Was this a trick of light in water? He reached his hand out to explore. He knew what he had forgotten that he knew.

Ke-wick

The fishes were an owl which flapped against the moon, not sun. The streaks of cirrus moved across familiar stars: Altair and Deneb and deep blue Vega. The waters were receding.

Ke-wick

Swiftly receding. Their sound rushed from his ears. The ocean was run dry. He sat upon its shore.

Teach us to sit still

Teach us to sit still. Help us to remember what we had forgotten that we knew.

That fearfulness grows to terror for being unexpressed
That many things cannot be spoken
That cannot be spoken means cannot be thought
That cannot means dare not
That it is not possible not to think, for knowledge is
      always secreted somewhere even if refused
That therefore the mind betrays itself
That therefore I am sick
That my sickness is universal

That there are vast empty voids between us
That Uncle Mory bought me a telescope
That a parsec is the interval at which half the axis of the
 earth's orbit subtends an angle of one second, this
 being useless information which cannot be
 dislodged from the brain
That this is beside the point
That this is, in fact, the way the brain functions,
 retaining what it will
That knowledge is always secreted somewhere even if
 refused
That therefore the mind betrays itself
That a man's reach exceeds his grasp
That Browning thought this proper
That nobody reads Browning any more
That Pippa, passing, saw God in his heaven, all right
 with the world
That God exceeds our grasp
That the world's a rough old place, mate, when all's
 said and done
That cigars make you ill
That pools make you wet
That water is laving
That water is encompassing
That I wish to be encompassed
That there are vast empty voids between us
That Uncle Mory bought me a telescope
That Betelgeux burns red
That a parsec is the interval at which half the axis of the
 earth's orbit subtends an angle of one second
That I have a mother

That the mind betrays itself
That I should have been a pair of ragged claws
That people still read Eliot, if only for his musical and
imagist delights since he has little to say to us in
other respects
That the delights of this world nevertheless exceed our
grasp
That the curled serrated greenness of a fresh elm leaf is
delightful
That sunlight on ripening wheat is delightful
That woodsmoke drifting among autumn trees is
delightful
That frost on stiff winter grass is delightful
That I love wet roads
That I love the smell of garlic
That I love the scream of swifts
That I love salt on my tongue
That Whitmanesque lists have reach but not grasp
That Eliot is the poet of infinite regret
That this statement is high-sounding but trite
That only the unimaginative have no regrets
That only the unimaginative have a grasp commensurate
with their reach
That cigars make you reach
That pools make you wet
That I cannot swim
That the mermaids will not sing to me
That I am gauche
That the easy give-and-take of human communication
is a mystery to me
That I am acutely aware of the vast empty voids

That my awareness is pathological

That my sickness is perhaps therefore not altogether
universal

That Uncle Mory bought me a telescope

That there are a hundred thousand million stars in the
Milky Way

That starfish are like stars

That I met Marguerite by a pool, crabbing

That I am horribly crabbed

That I do not dare to eat a peach

That the mind betrays itself

That the mind is, however, capable of great feats of
assimilation, sorting and storing the most arcane
of facts

That language has a neurological basis centred on the
left hemisphere of the brain

That Thomas Aquinas lived from 1226 until 1274 and
argued, in his *Summa Contra Gentiles*, that reason
and faith are compatible

That an Airedale is a breed of dog which originated in
Yorkshire bout 1850 as a cross of the otter hound
with Irish and Welsh terriers

That a parsec is the interval at which half the axis of the
earth's orbit subtends an angle of one second

That knowledge is dry

That though I have the gift of prophecy, and understand
all mysteries, and all knowledge; and though I
have all faith, so that I could remove mountains,
and have not charity, I am nothing

That I wish I could believe this

That I have a mother

That many things cannot be spoken
That I am dry
That I am nothing
That our lives prepare us lessons which we do not care
      to learn
That fearfulness grows to terror for being unexpressed
That to speak we first must listen
That I do not wish to listen
That I do not wish means do not dare
That I am not courageous
That some are born courageous while the rest of us
      must endure
That this is special pleading and highly regrettable
That I could doubtless argue sunrise into sunset through
      the cunning manipulation of words
That I do love words in all their glory
That I love Shoals because they shimmer in the
      shallows
That I love Celerity for how fast it runs
That I love Ginger-pop which fizzes
That I love Rigadoon, despite forgetting what it means
That I love Grackle, likewise
That words are the grappling hooks we use to span the
      empty voids between us
That the span is beyond our grasp
That this argument is becoming exclusively abstract
That the mind betrays itself
That a parsec is the interval at which half the axis of the
      earth's orbit subtends an angle of one second
That human kind cannot bear very much reality
That Eliot knew what he was talking about when he

wrote that, all right

That reality is another woolly abstract which embraces
    the entire physical and spiritual universe

That Uncle Mory bought me a telescope

That it's the physical which bothers Eliot

That it's the embraces in particular

That this is a scurrilous attack on a major literary figure
    of our time

That many things cannot be spoken

That I met Marguerite by a pool

That I have a mother

That knowledge is always secreted somewhere even if
    refused

That to shun the physical is to protect the psyche from
    oblivion

That this is pretentious

That I have no sense of humour at all

That I once told a joke involving a reindeer, a car
    mechanic and a packet of chewing gum and was
    unable to remember the punch-line

That it's a rum do, squire, and that's no mistake

That to shun the physical is indeed to protect the psyche

That the word Physical is imprecise

That a parsec is the interval at which half the axis of the
    earth's orbit subtends an angle of one second

That there are a hundred thousand million stars in the
    Milky Way

That human kind can bear but dull reality

That *Rangifer tarandus* is the only species of deer in
    which the females have antlers

That the typical modern motor car has a semi-monocoque

construction in which the body panels support the
    road loads

That propyl gallate is an antioxidant used in the
    manufacture of chewing gum

That the punch-line still evades me

That a man's reach exceeds his grasp

That to risk the physical is to risk the oblivion of the
    psyche

That to risk oblivion is a temptation

That many things cannot be spoken

That fearfulness grows to terror for being unexpressed

'What's undeniable,' Dalton Wymberley stated briskly, 'is that we can't have a strategically vital island like Cyprus at the mercy of squabbling, unstable natives.

'Not,' he added with a swift trawl of the eyes beyond his immediate circle, 'that we're allowed to express it in quite that fashion. Or to say that the despicable archbishop ought to be strung up from the nearest banyan tree, or whatever grows out there.'

'You'll soon find out.'

'All too soon. Tarquin, for God's sake!'

Wymberley, who held an insignificant portfolio in the foreign office, was about to accompany the prime minister on a British peace mission to the Mediterranean.

'An evil bastard, Makarios,' he opined contentedly, continuing in a louder voice but without any break whatsoever: 'Those trousers staying up all right?'

'Yes, thank you.'

'That young man over there is wearing a pair of my trousers. He had an adventure in the pool. Aren't you risking things a bit?' he boomed with a sharp laugh.

'I'll sit down, I think.'

'Come and join us.'

He joined them and was ignored. Wymberley and his party, half a dozen men of mature years, occupied a nest of canvas chairs a little way from the pool. Their presence ensured a certain sobriety. The young people in the water laboured slowly up and down with the frog-like motions of the breast stroke. When they came to rest, they spoke in little more than whispers, which nevertheless bounced off the surface and seemed to hang suspended in the night air for a few seconds before dying away.

'Back off, Jack. You're becoming insufferable.'

'I know you don't mean that.'

'You'd better believe it.'

The man closest to him began to talk of City matters, asking whether he had money to invest and recommending unit trusts. These were, apparently, as safe as houses.

'An excellent track record. Fine yields.'

There was a flurry of water, laughter, a swirl of bodies beneath the surface.

'She meant it, Jack.'

'If we don't sort this lot out, the Russians will.'

'Exactly my meaning. How do you think Krushchev would have reacted if this had been in his backyard.'

'Of course I meant it.'

'We'd have invaded within twenty-four hours, no doubt about it.'

'And capital appreciation, too. You can't do better.'

'Not really.'

'Had Grivas shot and at the very least put Makarios under lock and key.'

'Which he'd then have thrown away.'

'Yes, Jack. Really.'

'If you like I'll jot down a few suggestions. A thousand in each would be a good idea.'

'But we're forced to be diplomatic, God help us. Treating a violent rabble as if they were rational human beings. It's like training chimpanzees to read and write.'

How to know? How to know that what she said meant something else? Did it or didn't it? How to know Grivas should be shot? How to know Makarios a bastard? Why trust a man about unit trusts? When understanding oneself so difficult, that many things cannot be spoken, that the mind betrays itself, how grasp the world beyond?

'The end of the imperial dream, old boy.'

'Each one of these has a broad spread of equities.'

'I'd take the hint, Jack, if I were you.'

'Over my dead body.'

'I'll ask for your advice when I need it, Frankie.'

'If it's individual shares you're after, mind.'

'Tra-la-la!'

How grasp that otherness, however simply many seem to, their grasp and reach not incommensurate, this sickness not quite universal? How cross the dark empty voids?

'But I see that I'm confusing you.'

'Don't you dare!'

'Harold is perhaps a little inclined to softness, but the FO are firm.'

'Just take this list away with you.'

'They won't let him back away from it.'

'Well, bloody hell Tarquin, I certainly shan't, as long as I've any influence in the matter.'

'Here's my card.'

'Boys, boys!'

'Ring me sometime if you'd like me to act for you. It's a fixed commission.'

'No, boys!'

How read the signs, divine the meaning of a gesture, of a kindness in the eye, of a smile upon the lips? How understand the silent complicity of Anna, heaving herself from the tug of the water, mouthing at him the one word Help?

It was the crooked arm behind her that created the inevitability. It fixed the image. No, no, there was of course an image already fixed: it replicated that earlier image. It was as if a negative were held in front of a photograph, the outlines matching. It was like two shadows merging. It was a revenance. There was no escape from it. That beefy arm was not his own, but it dripped with water and it framed her face. The hair was blond and wet from her dip. He was haunted.

*

'Protect me,' she pleaded with a little laugh, throwing herself to the grass beside his chair. She was wearing a bikini of ruched cotton with a pattern of green and white checks. She spread her dress on the ground alongside her and unrolled a large towel, royal blue with the words HOTEL BELLA VISTA sunk into its pile. 'Someone over there has got the wrong idea.'

The moon was full in the sky. The lawn spread yellow beyond her.

'Where's Robin?'

'Gone home.' She stretched upon the towel. 'The very thought of swimming finished him off.'

A row of young men, four of them, stood along the rim of the pool, staring. There was menace in their eyes, and they rocked gently on the balls of their feet as if to keep some inner momentum going.

'He's terribly vain, you know. Couldn't abide the thought of having his ascetic figure ridiculed by *hoi polloi*.'

The sky was giddy with stars. He picked out Perseus and the sharp W of Cassiopeia, experiencing for the thousandth time how, when gazed upon, they seemed to blaze, to dim to pearly smudge, to kindle bright again. A speck of searing whiteness engraved an arc among the constellations and quickly died, to be followed immediately by another.

'Did you see that?' she asked, turning towards him. 'Wasn't that simply beautiful?'

'The Perseids.'

'Is that so? And could they collide with Earth?'

'Hardly. What you saw were no larger than grains of sand. Debris from space.'

That Uncle Mory bought me a telescope

'You're pretty knowledgeable, you know that,

164

Douglas?'

'Knowledge is dry.'

'Ha! Douglas O'Dale is a little dry, maybe. But that, I take it, is your famous English irony.'

Sometimes their hands touched under water as they swim. Their fingers would curl and cling. As if by accident. Their thighs would, inadvertently, touch. They would not hurry, they would not hurry to move away. They dare not look at one another in those moments

'I've never managed to get through to an Englishman yet.'

The four young men began to shuffle away, defeated by indifference, by time, by boredom, joshing among themselves for comfort.

'Not to the core, I mean. Not even my cousin Robin. Or especially not him, I suppose. In books it's different, of course. All my intimate English relationships are literary ones.'

She told him so, that nobody had called her Marguerite. Ever before, anybody. They loved hotly

'Did you ever fall in love with a character in a novel?'

'No. No, I don't think so.'

'When I was very young it was with dashing, rather dangerous men like Mr Rochester, naturally enough. In my grand maturity I like to think I've grown a lot more discerning, at least more appreciative of less obvious attributes. Nowadays I can even get the odd pang for an angry young man or a whisky priest.'

The top of her swimsuit stretched over full rounded breasts. *They dare not look* There was a freckled area high on the inside of one thigh, dark spots like a star-cluster, like the Pleiades. Tussocks of crinkled hair escaped the tightness of the material where it clutched her legs. The moon was full.

They fished in a pool

'And literary affairs tend to be more satisfying, don't they? None of life's mess about them when they're over.'

What if time not continuous but cyclical and we unaware of the periodicity, like ancients unable to predict a meteor's return, so that two moments may be in fact and against all commonsense appearance part of the one indivisible creative act, their seeming variance largely a product of our own incapacity for clear vision, we seeing through the clouded atmosphere of our own ignorance and maybe, too, at a distance, as we perceive the stars through light which left them aeons ago and they having moved, so that was actually exists is never quite as we see it and we must needs guess at what we find and agree, out of as much humility as we can muster, to be satisfied with approximations, faint recognitions that a time has come round again; and what if, though part of the one simultaneous creative act, these moments nonetheless should evolve, should burgeon, should hatch, like pupa into chrysalis then chrysalis on again, the different stages all the same moment, yet indivisible, but revealing new aspects of that moment, manifestations of its meaning, ever enriching it, explicating it, bringing it further towards the maturation whose seeds it already contains, it being entire unto itself; then we become thereby beholden

surely, recognising the synchronicity of the moment, ourselves inevitably a part of that moment, to partake of its essence, of its true expression, of its fulfilment, yielding ourselves up to that inevitability however bold the summons, however much the betraying mind may strive and strain against it

*

'I'm beginning to believe, Douglas, that Eliot is more your obsession than mine.'

They had wandered through the garden and arrived at a little lawn at the front of the house. Light poured from large sash windows and from French windows still open to the warm air of early morning. There was a drinks table, its cloth by now heavily stained with spillings of red wine, whisky and cocktails. Bateson, the Wymberleys' elderly gardener, was on duty in an ill-fitting dinner jacket, a staunch, bemused smile decorating his ruddy outdoor face with two rows of strong, misshapen teeth. Large moths careered among the guests, occasionally provoking outraged squeals from the women when they settled on clothing or fluttered close to their heads.

'Shantih agree with you.'

'I also think you're rather drunk.'

It was the sherry. He was unused to it, to any alcohol. Besides, he associated the drink with his aunts, sipping from little thimbles like mice nibbling cheese. It was quite impossible to believe that it had any strength. He was on his third glass, and Bateson poured generously.

Her skin was brown. She had thrown her dress over her

swimsuit, the buttons at the top still open. She wore leather sandals on her feet.

˙ 'But to answer your question, I do remembered most of what he said in that lecture. Among other things, he spoke about Goethe. You've read him in the German, no doubt.'

He nodded, holding out his glass for another refill. The metal sculpture on the lawn seemed to gleam more brightly than before, the horseman to ride his steed with greater energy.

'One up to Douglas. Well, Eliot's had a re-think about Goethe just recently, which is very interesting. The man, he now grants, was a sage. Most generous of him, don't you think?'

'Before that?'

'Oh, he couldn't stand him. Said he dabbled in philosophy and poetry and didn't make much of a fist of either. Even Goethe's famous healthiness was reckoned to be artificial. Priggish was the word he used. Of course I suggest that Elio was simply frightened of that robust health. Your poet of infinite regret regretted that he wasn't able to experience so much so deeply. That's the littleness I was referring to.'

Sherry was sweet and heavy. It left a memory on the tongue. It sang songs in the brain.

'What's brought about the revaluation I can't imagine. He's suddenly discovered wisdom in Goethe. A native gift of intuition, he finds, is ripened by experience. The German sage understands the nature of living things, especially the human heart. I must say it gives me quite a shiver to hear Eliot talk about the human heart.'

'Perhaps you don't allow sufficiently for the capacity of

people to change.'

'Says he with such slow emphasis that he *must* have been drinking too much. Do put that glass down, Douglas, before you disgrace yourself.'

'With a steady hand. See?'

'Bravo!'

Toe-nails painted nearly pink. Such sweet toes. And slender ankles.

'You may be right, but he's left if very late in the day, that's all I can say. Eliot's whole life has been a struggle to reveal and not to reveal. He's like Odysseus, hearing those siren voices and wanting to hear them, but making sure he's so securely bound that his response is never more than partial. He yearns and he quivers, that is, but he'll never be set free. He won't actually visit those sirens, God no!'

'A survival instinct.'

'Or he's Sisyphus, for ever pushing away at that boulder. That's his writing, the pushing. He gets the dead weight of his fear a few yards up the slope every time he picks up the pen, but the energy runs out in no time at all. He's flattened again.'

She laughed, a laugh suspended in the air while she continued to talk. *That he had a mother. That he met Marguerite by a pool*

'So I'm fascinated by this human heart business. Perhaps he'll eventually come to see that his original antipathy to Goethe came from a reading of Faust. You may interrupt if you like.'

'I shouldn't know where to begin.'

'Nonsense. I'm sure you know the work very well.'

'Yes, I do, but I can't pretend to find it as profound as I rather think I should.'

'Being awe-struck is hardly a useful critical stance, surely?'

He was, for a moment, more concerned with his physical stance. He always thought more clearly while walking. They had been standing in the one place for many minutes, and when he took a step forward he seemed to have no knowledge of where his foot would land.

'Sin,' he said baldly.

'Go on.'

'It seems to me that Faust is merely playing at it.'

She walked close to him. They threaded between the inter ring of guests and began a leisurely patrol around the perimeter of the lawn.

'His pact with Mephistopheles does allow him unbridled licence.'

'That's my point exactly,' he said. 'What does he do, given that freedom? What terrible sins does he commit? He eats and drinks a little, plays a few silly tricks on his enemies.'

'And seduces an innocent girl. Can't we call that a genuine sin, Douglas?' She grinned. 'But no, it's probably the kind of thing you do every day.'

He waved her to silence, urgently, then stood still for a few moments seeking the proper words.

'That's not the ultimate sin, is it?'

'He murders someone, too.'

'But these are commonplaces, Anna, can't you see? This isn't someone you read about in the Sunday papers, some low ruffian in trouble with the law yet again. It's Faust, the brilliant man who sold his soul to the Devil. Can't he do —'

The thought was difficult.

'Better, were you going to say?'

'No, no, but there's a knowledge that he shouldn't have. Or perhaps he should have the knowledge and then betray it. Don't ask me what it is. I don't know what it is, but that's what true evil would be. Perhaps it's inexpressible.'

'Something secret?'

'Yes, perhaps. I really don't know.'

They walked on in silence for a while. Now and then he felt her bare arm rub against his elbow. The people around them did not exist.

'That's what Eliot almost saw,' she said at last. 'You remember the precise compact Faust make with Mephistopheles? He'll lose his soul once he reaches the moment of supreme happiness and cries out *Ah, still delay – thou art so fair*!'

'In the Bayard Taylor translation.'

'Thanks, professor. I suppose you could quote me half a dozen. But that supreme moment is the point Eliot so often approaches and always backs off from. His whole life is a treading close to the abyss and then retreating. His dislike of Goethe is a recognition that, in Faust, he tries to name the unnameable – and descends to the commonplace, just as you suggest. Goethe has crudely spilled the beans, whereas in Eliot you get only suppression, the powerful hint. It's after a rare mention of the human heart, come to think of it, that he most nearly says what he means. In *The Waste Land*, when he writes about the awful daring of a moment's surrender.'

'By this, and this only, we have existed. But he didn't mean mere existence, did he? Something vital.'

'It's orgasm, of course, but I guess it's your secret knowledge, too. I think we're in agreement on this, Douglas. You're permitted another drink on the strength of it.'

Bateson poured two large sherries, tirelessly smiling. It was two o'clock. The moths fluttered madly in the lights from the house and another shooting star burned itself to a bright ember in the cold grate of the sky.

Thou shalt not presume

Thou shalt not covet

Thou shalt not violate

Thou shalt not do that which it is unseemly to do

Thou shalt not be insufferably mealy-mouthed about
that which it is unseemly to do

Thou shalt not obey thy baser instincts

Thou shalt not use this commandment to hide from
thyself what is most base within thyself which
may be other than instinctual

Thou shalt not, *e.g.*, basely equivocate

Thou shalt not yield to base fear

Thou shalt not, moreover, disguise base fear as moral
imperative

Thou shalt not basely consider thyself different from
other men which means superior or at the very
least more sensitive and discriminating

Thou shalt not deny that which it is sin to deny
Thou shalt not think only in terms of shalt nots
Thou shalt affirm life
Thou shalt remember now thy Creator in the days of
thy youth
Thou shalt therefore in so doing pray for strength to
affirm life
Thou shalt honour thy mother that thy days may be
long upon the land
Thou shalt dare to eat a peach
Thou shalt be honest
Thou shalt be honest with thyself
Thou shalt not use this commandment to convince
thyself that all that which thou dost shall be honest
Thou shalt not covet
Thou shalt affirm life
Thou shalt seize the moment
Thou shalt not descend to sloganising
Thou shalt not violate
Thou shalt rise above petty moralising which is nothing
more than convention in its Sunday best
Thou shalt distrust the glib use of language even if
perpetrated by thyself
Thou shalt distrust the glib use of language especially is
perpetrated by thyself
Thou shalt nevertheless believe in language
Thou shalt honour its reach
Thou shalt honour its grasp which is almost commensurate
Thou shalt honour its wit
Thou shalt honour its beauty
Thou shalt honour thy mother that thy days be long

Thou shalt not presume
Thou shalt not possess knowledge which it is forbidden
    to possess
Thou shalt not pact with Mephistopheles
Thou shalt pray for strength
Thou shalt not deny that which it is sin to deny
Thou shalt dare the awful moment
Thou shalt by this have existed
Thou shalt not violate
Thou shalt affirm life
Thou shalt not violate
Thou shalt affirm

Were these the ways that lovers always used – the tremulous silences, the tentative declarations, the desultory exchanges of inconsequential intimacies?

They patrolled the garden slowly, as in a dream. Sometimes they took a path away from the lights of the house, into the darkness of trees, wandering blindly until eventually they met a track they had walked before or emerged by a lawn or a tennis court where, they were vaguely aware, other people were talking and laughing and drinking, though not, surely, at quite this time and in quite this place. They made no conscious decisions about their route, but seemed to turn always at the same moment as if their very instincts were in tune.

She came from Pennsylvania. Her father was a farmer, apparently of the amateur kind since he seemed to find ample time to indulge his hobbies of restoring steam engines and collecting glass. He was an authority on both. Her mother was descended from a line of Calvinist preachers, whose excesses of rigour she pardoned with surprising good nature considering that her own temperament was altogether more light and lenient.

'My mother was the first ripe fruit on a withered old tree,' Anna smiled. 'That was a piece of luck for me.'

'You were spoiled?'

'Indulged, maybe. That doesn't sound quite so awful, does it? She had her standards, of course, but she wasn't going to put her children through the black torments she'd known herself. If she ever disapproves of what I do, I rarely know it.'

'Do you give her reason, do you think?'

'Ah!'

She laughed. She had a lovely laugh, a guttural explosion climbing the scale by three light notes with the merest hint of a fourth.

They spoke of early memories. Hers were of picnics in the Allegheny mountains with her two younger brothers. There was a family ritual on the first proper day of spring, when the brilliant sun of early morning fizzled against the new leaves of a stand of birch trees and the brook chuckled past the breakfast room full and cold. Then they would harness her favourite old horse to a large haywain which had at some time been crudely painted in bright reds, blues and yellows and which, in these days of tractors and trailers, was used solely for festive occasions. Somehow everyone knew that the moment had arrived. Hampers would appear fully packed, friends would swing in at the gate with large bottles protruding from backpacks, and in no time at all the cart would be swaying along the rutted tracks towards the far hills, her mother and father perched on the board at the front and a boisterous army of young people happily tossed this way and that in the back.

'No,' he said, 'I have no brothers or sisters.'

Dalton Wymberley, still by the pool with his cronies, waved a cigar in his direction but did not mention the trousers.

She spoke of life on the farm, its sounds and its smells. They kept cows, and as a young girl she liked to stand silently in the stalls, watching the breath from their nostrils, hearing their teeth tirelessly chewing. Later, at an age when she often felt the need to retreat into her own private world, she would climb the ladder to the loft above the cattle and lie on the straw with a book, reading for hours in the dust-hung light of the small window while the heavy creatures below fed, snorted, passed water, clattered their feet.

'Did you have animals around you, Douglas?'

'Nothing more than a Persian cat next door. Mine was a suburban upbringing. Neat hedges and rose beds.'

'What did your father do?'

'I didn't have a father.'

'Oh, I'm sorry. And your mother?'

The path led under a pergola and then divided. They took the darker way, beneath a row of horse chestnuts. The green fruit hung above them like tiny globe lanterns.

'Did she raise you by herself?'

'With relatives. Life was difficult for her.'

They walked on in silence. He felt not completely in

charge of himself. His thoughts were not under their usual strict control, but seemed to arrive at his lips already fully formed so that he became, in a way, a spectator of himself. Yet for some reason this did not alarm him. He submitted to it.

'She was a delightful woman, intelligent and vivacious. When she entered a room everyone noticed her and all conversation stopped. She could have chosen any role in life and made a success of it.'

'How wonderful!'

'Yes, wonderful. She was warm and considerate, too. As a mother she was everything that one could have wished.'

The croquet players were still at their wicked sport. A ball came flying off the green and splashed into the gravel at their feet. Someone stretched across to retrieve it, apologising.

'She never once spoke a cruel word, ever, and was always ready with an encouragement.'

He heard himself say these things and was satisfied with them. They sounded right.

'She worked, your mother?'

'An actress. A very fine actress. It came naturally to her, perhaps because of the attention she always received. Adulation almost. Life itself was one of her performances, if you like, and she never fluffed her lines.'

Was that an echo of something? He didn't care.

'And she . . .' Anna began, her voice suddenly faltering. When she tried again it was in a softer tone. 'She's dead?'

'What, my mother?'

'You seemed to speak as if. I imagined that.'

'No, she's quite alive. I don't see her very often now, that's all.'

They paused by the house for another drink. Anna sipped an orange juice, but he chose sherry again, watching greedily as Bateson filled the schooner to the brim. Waiting, they chatted idly with people they had met before, but nothing could break the spell. He hardly heard what was said or what he said until he was alone with her again.

During their third lap of the garden, walking more slowly than ever, they talked of childhood adventures (falling from a horse, scrumping, skating on thin ice), and progressed by way of likes and dislikes (cherry pie, tapioca, the smell of cut grass, Sunday school) to friends and enemies. She began, that done, to recall first loves.

'When I was about nine years old I was all a-tremble for a boy called Dino Brown. It was something about his nose. Sort of proud, I think. It can't have been only his nose, presumably, but that's what I remember now. He held his head erect and the nose marched out in front. His father taught in the local school. Dino was the first boy I ever held hands with. We used to walk home from school together. One day he told me he'd hurt his wrist and so unfortunately couldn't manage it, and I was smart enough to realise that maybe something wasn't quite right. Especially when he turned down my eminently logical suggestion of switching sides, me holding his good hand. That, I'm afraid, was the beginning of the end.'

'It broke your heart?'

'For several days, I think. Now it's your turn.'

'I beg your pardon?'

'To reveal the history of your infantile passions. I insist, Douglas. Let there be no vital secrets between us.'

The four young men from the pool swaggered towards them. They bowed exaggeratedly in Anna's direction and she waved a dismissive hand at them, though smiling all the time. He averted his gaze.

'On holiday once,' he said.

How could he tell it? He felt how grossly redundant an explanation would be, a superfetation of the one indivisible moment.

'Is that all I'm to get? Come, sir! Age?'

'Oh, about twelve I suppose.'

'Place?'

'The Isle of Wight.'

'Sounds magical, wherever it may be. Sand and sea? Blue skies?'

'Yes. Yes, it was just like that.'

'And the girl. This is serious research, Douglas. I need the name for my files.'

'Margaret.'

How difficult it was to speak the name! It was almost a profanation. The true name, *Marguerite, Marguerite* echoed and echoed inside his head.

'I think you should tell me next how you met.'

'By a pool,' he replied in staccato fashion. 'Crabbing.'

'Very good. Let's move on to a description. My, you make this hard work! White Caucasian?'

'Blonde.'

'Pretty?'

'Well, perhaps. Probably. Somewhat freckled.'

'This isn't very flattering you know, for the first love of

your life. Though I suppose it's better than the proud nose. You can't persuade your memory to make her pretty?'

'But it's not a question of — ' How could this be expressed? 'If someone matters so much, it's not important — '

He could not express it.

'I shall take her prettiness as read, whatever you say. Someone has to stand up for the fair sex. This was a brief holiday romance, I take it?'

'If you like.'

'And afterwards, nothing?'

Afterwards nothing?

'Nothing.'

The guests were beginning to thin out. There was nobody in the white plastic chairs where he had sat with the Harbins. When they passed the lawn with the equestrian sculpture they saw Bateson alone at his drinks table, tilting the remains of a brandy bottle to his lips.

She spoke of teenage amours now, chuckling over episodes which must surely have occasioned grief or embarrassment at the time.

'Ted Cernick's father had a beautiful pink and cream Packard convertible, and Ted borrowed it to drive me to the Susquehanna River one Saturday night. Least, he *said* he'd borrowed it. There was some question about this afterward. He wanted to show me a place he sometimes fished. That was the official version. We parked by a little creek, and he was just whispering me a few fancy things he was sure I'd want to hear, and which I wasn't too averse to hearing if the truth be known, when the earth began to move for something other than the usual reason.

He'd left the thing out of gear and with the handbrake off, too. We rolled very, very gently towards the water, and poor Ted had time to leap out but no time at all to do anything about it. I sat where I was and shut my eyes, and the water came about two feet up the sides before the vehicle came to rest.'

He glanced furtively at her from time to time as they walked. Yes, prettiness was irrelevant. She wasn't pretty, but she had grace of movement. He liked the pressure of her thighs against her cotton dress.

'And since, Mr Dry-as-dust O'Dale, you're obviously going to keep a close guard on your youthful indiscretions, I shall proceed to tell you about The Great Pennsylvania Tobacco Fraud.'

Underneath her dress she wore her two-piece swimsuit. He wondered whether it was still damp and clinging.

'Not that I can explain its intricacies, which defeated me even then. It was something to do with tax avoidance, and with warehouses of the stuff which were never legally declared.'

He imagined how it might be damp and clinging, and he saw again the movement of her thighs against the cotton of her light dress.

'I'd been dating this policeman, Robert Fresco. Bobby was good-looking in a Kirk Douglas kind of way, strong and very tall. I've always liked tall men. Oh, and with an irresistible dimpled chin. He seemed the very model of good health and uprightness. Unfortunately he was also married. I didn't quite know that at the time, if you understand me. I didn't want to know.'

They took a path they had not come across before. It

ran alongside a yew hedge and emerged on a drive which swung around the house and came to an end here, well behind it. It was overhung by a spreading cedar tree, and the blazing moon cast deep shadows over a large car which sat outside a wooden lock-up.

'Bobby liked to be a mystery man, full of secrets he couldn't possible divulge to me. One night, after we'd been to a movie, we drove out to one of these warehouses and he disappeared inside for the best part of an hour. He seemed pretty excited afterwards, but I didn't think anything of it.'

They stopped by the car, a Rolls Royce Silver Cloud. Through the trees he could hear the thin sounds of the skiffle music.

'It turned out that wholesome Bobby was taking a rake-off from the criminals. Some honest cop! He tried to use me as an alibi for the night he'd been out there. Can you imagine the difficulty? What would you have done?'

'I don't know.'

She put a hand to the silver statuette on the car's bonnet. The Spirit of Ecstasy. Underneath was her two-piece swimsuit.

'I simply told the truth. It's a funny thing, but for a while I liked him even more after that.' She laughed. 'The perversity of the human heart. This is Wymberley's, isn't it?'

Wymberley's car. Were these the ways that lovers used, speaking banalities while the heart surged, smiling blandly while the blood pounded? He found the words so very difficult.

'Not perverse, no. If somehow,' he said, 'of the essence. Vital, I mean. If part of.'

'Just look at this!'

Shc peered through the driver's window, seeing how the moon lit up the burnished wood of the fascia, the dials with their dark, mysterious hands, the leather upholstery.

'Those loves.' He was standing behind her now, stooping to look through the window, feeling his chest touch upon her shoulder-blade. Surging heart, pounding blood. 'Need not be.' Was it sill damp and clinging, the swimsuit? 'Not dead, necessarily. Not if.'

'If we treasure them like lockets of hair? I do believe you're a romantic at heart, Douglas.'

'Treasure, yes. Yes, but more.'

His fingers were on the rear door handle, and when he pressed down on it the door swung open. He could smell the leather.

'What luxury!'

She pushed past him and sat inside, sinking into the softness of the seat, her smile almost triumphant.

'Do you know, Douglas, I've never been inside one of these beauties before.'

Were these the ways? First come the dumb acknowledgements, the pantomime of senses intertwined. Follow the fumbling consonants, stuck syllables, crude dialogues that falter. Next might it be – oh chapters of desire, oh stations of the cross! – the cautious overtures, the tender broachings.

'Anna,' he said.

She was inside. He put his knee upon the seat and leaned towards her.

'Anna.'

And her eyes said yes to him, he would always swear

they did, as he put his face close to hers, *yes* they said in a way that he surely could not possibly misunderstand *yes yes I will Yes*

*

however later long reflection might instruct, reshape, deny, yet *yes* her eyes said as he touched her, as his fingers found her hair and took it gently like a sifting, pulling, mussing, stroking.

'Douglas.'

Heard his name above the thunder in his ears, Douglas, saying. *Dug lass*

'Anna.'

Dug lass oh dare

Smelled the smell of her close to, some musky odour.

'Now, now.'

Know, know

Musky odour, tang of chlorine, stench of leather.

'Please.'

Oh please, oh please, oh please, oh please

He stroked her cheek, so soft, so warm. He took her face within his hands. A fragile thing.

'Misunderstand.'

Not what I meant at all, at all. That is not it, at all

'The moment, don't you see,' he said. 'Redeemed. The time redeemed.'

He toppled forward, pressed his mouth against the flesh above her breast.

'No.'

Know

'No, Douglas, no.'

If one should say That is not it

'Regret,' hearing her say. 'You will regret.'

The smell close to. Musk in the nose. Sweet body warmth.

Regret. Regress

Her suppleness, the body writhing.

Blood shaking my heart

'Marguerite,' he muttered. 'My Marguerite.'

'You're crazy.'

'But you're my lovely Marguerite.'

She could not see, did not yet know the role she played. He laughed within to think the moment ripening, his hands upon her shoulders, tugging at the cotton.

'In God's name, Douglas.'

Why God torment unless indeed we may yet grasp

He felt the cotton fabric tear. He pulled the dress from off her shoulders. Her bosom heaved. Whence came his strength? The dress was a rag he tossed aside.

'Dear Marguerite.'

'I'll scream, damn you.'

The epileptic on the bed curves backward, clutching at her sides

He held her arms against her flanks and sank upon her, his chest against her mouth. It was not right that she should scream.

'Oh my love, my dear, my Marguerite.'

The swimsuit bottom was not wet.

Craving

She bit him hard then, very hard. He started back, his hand upon the wound.

'Bastard,' she said.

185

She did not know the role she played. The thunder sounded in his head and he flung her back against the seat.

'It's the moment,' he cried. 'Don't you see?'

He wrenched the garment down her legs and looked upon the secret thing he never once had known before, that mythical, sacred thing. He took its tangled mound in rough and urgent fingers and she stiffened and lay still.

Time not continuous but cyclical

His free hand released his waist band, worked upon the flies, lowered the trousers. He was shaking, but fierce. It was a power he had not known.

'Marguerite,' he said. 'Anna.'

'Oh, you bastard,' she said, and she twisted round and bit his upper arm so that the pain shot across his chest and ran down to his loins.

He struck her instinctively, not very hard, no, not hard at all, not a blow to pain as much as to shock *having never slapped, himself never slapped* and she fell back and he sprawled upon her.

Gal's alps, lap, lapse

Body heat, musk, an almost foetid stench that inflamed him. He felt a heavy ache in that great swelling which he now guided with his hand towards her.

'Darling.'

Her eyes were closed, her face screwed up as if in pain, but the blow was not hard, not vicious.

'Let me.'

She would not let, but he pushed against her, dipped her shoulders down into the leather of the seat, forced her knees open with his own.

186

Awful daring, the awful daring

He thrust, not knowing where. He battered until he broke inside her.

She wept.

'Dear Marguerite.'

Her fingernails were tearing at his flesh but he could not stop.

Craving

The delicious friction of his engorged vein against the roof of her passage, how it maddened him!

Affirm, thou shalt affirm

He slid as deep as he could go and cleaved to her a moment, fast embedded *where the tides do not reach* pinning her flailing arms, holding himself deep, deep inside.

Whimpering, she.

'My lovely.'

And now he part pulled himself away, and sank, and rose and sank, and felt the moment ripening *by this to have existed* he felt the moment ripening.

He saw the glowing ball of Betelgeux.

Affirm, affirm, affirm

Darting fish in a limpid pool.

Mermaids.

Do not reach where the tides

Mermaids attempting to sing.

He clawed in desperation at her body, rocked inside her helpless body, rasped his frantic cock against her body until the gathering store of semen burst and swam.

*16 Continent to the letter, as before - causing
pathological linguistic impotence (8)*

An unfair setting. This word is to be found only in
obscure dictionaries of psychology.

17 Personal resolution does feel justified (4-2-2)

What do the fools who gawp and titter know about the contemplative life? Look at those funny creatures in their cowls and sandals, they gibber. How sadly remote they are from the bustling world outside their safe retreat. The *real* world, they mean. The one they so fruitfully inhabit themselves.

Escaping, of course. Fleeing something. Grief, perhaps, or shame. The notion of a positive commitment is quite beyond these wretched imbeciles. Something terrible must have happened to make a man hide himself away from his wise, good-natured, so evidently winsome fellow beings.

Very well: let them produce a single man or woman who has suffered no tragedy, no private cataclysms of wrong-doing or separation or loss. They can't, of course. It's the human condition. And how many of these benighted sufferers have considered, for even one fleeting moment, adopting the solitary life?

Practically none, is the answer.

Contemplatives run towards, not away from. They need none of your insolent commiserations, thank you very much. They aren't cripples. Keep your smug condolences to yourself.

And how complacently these morons assess their jejune vision of the tranquility they imagine to exist inside. Absolutely charming for a few days, no doubt, my dear. (They have no sane doubts at all, the clowns.) The peace would be divine, but the boredom . . .

Let them try it. Men have been broken in that silence.

Prayer is the monk's special business. It's what he's for. He prays for all mankind. What do you begin to know of the agonies of his supplications? What can you guess of his spiritual exhaustions? You know nothing. To hell with your colourful pageants of tonsured misfits.

Your busy life is more complicated? Simpleton! More strenuous? Gadfly! More worthwhile? Wastrel! You swell with pride for managing the great world's weighty affairs? Buffoon! Try dealing with the Godhead.

Try kneeling for hours at a time, for days at a time, with little break for rest or food, imploring His presence. Try that, you dribbling loon, then mouth some pat platitude about God in his Heaven.

Do you understand me?

Try praying your brain to a stupor; try chanting; try singing praises; try poring over every last line in every last book of theology; try confession; try flagellation; try seeking Him out in nature; try ignoring Him; try shouting loudly into the void; try closing up your eyes and ears; try ridding your brain of the lightest thought; try starvation; try stilling the words in your head.

Do you understand what I say, blockhead? That there is no limit to a man's depravity. That his rapacity knows no bounds. That he may even in his madness, in the obscene extremity of his passion, attempt a monstrous act of rape upon the living God!

19 Plumb the depths of human tragedy for a spell (6)

Let's keep calm.

It is a beautiful morning. The low March sun squints inquisitively into my sturdy log cabin, lighting upon the print of Niagara Falls on the wall above my bed. My bed. I have been here for some weeks now, and may surely claim reasonable use of the possessive adjective. Indeed, I am constantly urged to regard everything within comfortable walking distance as if it were a kind of temporary inheritance: 'All this is yours, Douglas. Enjoy! Grab one of our golf buggies and hammer that little white ball into submission. Use the sauna as often as you like. You could do with some colour. Why not take a boat out on the lake?'

My desk, too, therefore, although I acknowledge that the imagined scroll-top is, in humdrum reality, nothing more substantial than a poorly jointed deal table with one leg shorter than the others, infuriatingly shorter, and that its assigned place in life is not under this large window but between the cooker and the refrigerator in the dinette. Or have I invented that word? A year in America instructs that all things are possible lexicon-wise. At first I was appalled, but I have come to realise the severity of this reaction. Anyone who reveres the language must surely feel astonished by its grotesque malleability, invigorated by its desperate freshness, amused by its curious distortions, consoled by its ability to survive each brute manipulation, and appalled.

Who am I to talk, however? A man who got the sack for his wordy waywardness.

Let me here apologise for the turn this manual has taken. Perhaps you feel rarely privileged, as you certainly should: not every compiler provides such a thorough diagnosis of his clues at whatever cost to himself. The instruction is, however, somewhat haphazard. If I had time I would, with benefit of hindsight, write a separate, slimmer volume, with handy lists and an index. Might cartoons perhaps enliven it?

I have no time.

The letter, when at last it came, was suitably impersonal. I had visited the newspaper offices perhaps half a dozen times in all those years. Never once had I spoken to the grand editor of the *Times* himself, whoever he was, nor for a moment had I wished to. He had dictated the dismissal, no doubt, but a secretary had then drawn her name all over the typewritten version of his with a large and childish hand, and with a *p.p.* which could only be interpreted as *pathetic personage*. Or *preternaturally puerile*, perhaps. Or *piddling peon*.

I toyed with the possibilities for some time before re-reading the death sentence.

I had known that it was coming, of course. All that talk about the need to make economies was so much clap-trap. Were they going to do away with the crossword puzzle? Of course not: the very suggestion would provoke commotion on the streets, the collapse of the London stock market and the fall of the government. Were they paying me more than anyone else? Impossible. My fee had not risen in five years. He was very sorry, he wrote.

Great service. Unrivalled expertise. Much valued. Utter clap-trap from that satrap.

A single clue undid me. I remember the moment vividly. It was a winter evening, the weather bitterly cold, and I had retired to bed early with an unfinished puzzle propped in front of me, a flask of coffee on my bedside table and a hot water bottle between my thighs. I wore a maroon dressing-gown with yellow lapels over my thickest pair of pyjamas, my head was topped by a black woollen hat and the uniform was completed by a pair of knitted navy blue mittens. I always wrote in pencil, an HB, the kind I am using now. These are trivial matters, but it seems to me that the glories and horrors of life, the moments of sudden recognition of awful presentiment, invariably have a banal setting

One clue remained to be set, for *Missal*: not a difficult task, although the relative shortage of equivalents does narrow the options. I was beginning to doze off, rogue syllables sporting in my brain with their accustomed promiscuousness, when the words seemed to write themselves on the paper.

It occurs to me that at this point the reader may care to experiment. Let this be the test of what you have learned! Devise a clue of your own for *Missal*. Shall we allow ten minutes? Please look away and set to work while I make a few suggestions:

– we might use an *s* for Bob and *mal* in its sense of 'ill' or 'badly'. So, for example, Is Bob taken in badly by prayer-book?

– or we might take advantage of the different meanings

of 'mass', as in Mass dismissal at the end.

– various hidden-word possibilities arise, among them the rather fetching *Martin Amis, Salman Rushdie collaboration produces religious book.*

– and there are straightforward anagrams: *Islam's prayer-book?* Yes, Yes, I do like that one.

How did you get on? This is the O'Dale scoring system: a point for each clue fairly set; an extra five points for each one which stimulated or amused you; another ten points for personal resonance.

A cheery wave from the owner of this leisure park. For me, of course, not for you. I raise an arm in salute. He enjoys English understatement and would disapprove should I give his own heartiness an answering bellow. He appears to be savaging scraps of paper with a spike just now, but I daresay a visit is imminent. He likes to talk about the property he sells and to ask my opinion, if only rhetorically. If pressed, I should have to offer *caveat emptor* as the most sensible advice.

Missal. The words which my pencil wrote unaided were seemingly innocuous, using 'MI' as the motorway and the remaining letters as a distortion of 'lass'. They were, in any case, the merest suggestion of the direction in which a clue might be developed. How this one was later resolved I cannot recall, but I do know that I did not accomplish it that same night. No further work was done that night. I sat as in a trance, my back stiff, my breath a thin cloud in the air of the unheated bedroom, the rubber bottle between my legs turned cold, my papers scattered on the floor. Waking next morning slightly nauseous and with an ache over one eye, I saw that I had pressed so hard with the pencil that the words seemed engraved upon the paper: *Take route to wronged girl.*

You see how it is? A dry and withered chrysalis sun-warmed, which splinters, revealing a pair of crumpled yet insistent wings; an ancient, buried seed, plough-turned and watered to green sprouting; a crossword clue which sifts and breaks and spills its long-stored treacheries. How stealthily the past pursues its restless narratives!

Calm. Let's keep calm.

No, I don't pretend that I had forgotten, of course not. There are memories we carry with us like facial blemishes the morning mirror is careful not to see. What would it serve to notice them? Who would benefit? This is not cowardice but prudence. I had been prudent. I had been prudent for more than thirty years, God knows, but after that night the husk began to crack. I could hear it all the time, a busy high-pitched crepitation, opening deep fissures into the past.

It was, I suppose, the element of command in the words which did the damage, the assumption that there was unfinished business to be done. A course of action for the coarse of action, as it were. (I apologise for the first and last time. This is my sickness, my necessity, my delight.) As those dormant recollections began to stir and swarm, the possibility of seeing Anna again burgeoned from a notion into a plan of campaign. What had been a furtive, tremulous desire had become, almost unknown to myself, an imperative.

A gentle word at this juncture for readers addicted to detective stories: the glamour is utterly bogus. I'm truly sorry if this shatters your illusions but, believe me, researching anything whatsoever is tiresome and largely unrewarding. Ah, you say, your experience is narrow and bookish. Not so. Here in America, for instance, where sad necessity has acquainted me with criminal investigations of the most sordid kind, the strain suffered by police officers can be measured in terms of their susceptibility to alcoholism, drug-taking, mental breakdown and divorce. Life's tough on those mean streets, baby!

My early attempts to trace 'the wronged girl', if rather less injurious to health, were exhausting and frustrating in the extreme. Who had known her during her two years in England? The most obvious leads ushered me into blind alleys. Pale, emaciated cousin Robin, apparently tougher than he looked, had taken up hang-gliding in his thirties and had, one glorious day of winking sun and nudging thermals, plummeted two hundred feet to his death on the South Downs. The aged parents who mourned him had by now taken flight from this world themselves, their little nest-egg given to charity in the absence of further offspring.

The Wymberley connection drew a more predictable blank. I had not expected a reply from the former politician himself (the rent-boy scandal and his consequent divorce had turned him into a shambling recluse somewhere unvisited in the Orkneys), but I was soon satisfied by others that she must have been at the party merely through the general invitation to village residents, permanent or otherwise. A tour of the locality failed to unearth anyone with more than the faintest memory of her.

All the while that I hunted, my compilation were growing more obscure, more fanatical . . .

Yes, yes, I beg your pardon! Remiss of me. I do know the question that burns a hole in your tongue, just as it inflamed mine, but what better demonstration of the bitter agonies which attend research? It was, alas, quite impossible to discover whether, when the longed-for moment arrived, the egregious Herbert Harbin did get his hands, and his board, on Dalton Wymberley's property. I sincerely hope not, don't you?

My compilations, in short, were once again a worry to that great organ of the English establishment. What its readers saw as a sorry deterioration, although I of course knew otherwise, was at first intermittent and rarely remarked upon. The occasional disgruntled letter was easy to ignore. Why had the word 'Missal' been set in four consecutive puzzles? (A mark of cunning, I informed the crossword editor: the clues were all different.) Why, indeed, was there a plethora of religious references? (A passing theme: next year, the lives and works of the great engineers.) Why were the clues getting longer? (Was there, I countered innocently, a problem over the cost of the printing ink?)

They had grown tortuous, I see now, because I was using the puzzle as an extension of the Personal Ads column. This was not a conscious act. Certainly I realised that the private nature of my references threatened to render the clues unsolvable, but when I flick through the file today I feel again not only the ruthlessness of my obsession but the rank despair of the amateur private eye. Grouped close together on the one grid would be significant words and phrases (open-air party; swimming pool; Cyprus; Tarquin) which might, must might, tempt some sharp-eyed, keen-witted reader to dash his memories down on paper and send them in to me. Or *hers*. Did I perhaps nourish the hope that by some happy chance she herself might be in England, time on her hands, tackling the *Times* crossword? The evidence suggests as much. Sometimes detailed statements and searching questions would be yoked in neighbouring clues of great complexity: *Man long ago violently held Anna with little return*, for instance, proceeding to *I've a sly, pointless conundrum – where is she?* (The pointless and therefore grossly inadequate solutions were 'neanderthal' and 'Sylvia', and I blush.) On one daring, impertinent occasion I even tucked her full name into the folds of a hidden-word clue.

This madness was, I say, some time in the maturing. After six months the paper was receiving perhaps two or three letters per puzzle. Another three months and the tally had trebled. A mere fortnight later there were fifty complaints for a single compilation, a house record I believe, and the writing on the wall was not in the least cryptic. As it happened, however, my luck had already turned. The fever had abated. By the time the Dear Doug letter arrive I was able to treat it as a kind of portent.

I had, you see, received another letter. Out of the dark blue, as it were. Her Oxford college, an obvious source of information, had initially seemed to be of no use at all. The principal sent me an address in America which proved to be uselessly out of date and, in a subsequent communication, regretted the insufficiency of her records, the debility of her mind, which was unable to summon any memories of the young lady in question, and the paucity of her suggestions for tracing her. Since her complacent latinisms had evidently claimed more of her energies than any useful searching, I was surprised to discover that she had, at least, taken the trouble to relay my request to former students through the college magazine. Enter briefly, and some ten months later, Jennifer Crown, spinster of the parish of Stourton Caundle, Dorset . . .

First, however, The Big Cover Up. The reader will understand that it would not be proper to reveal Anna's full name to the size of public likely to buy this long-awaited work. The reader will certainly understand once the events yet to be related have been fully digested. I shall take the liberty, therefore, of changing her name and those of any other American citizens I mention who might possibly have their reputations damaged by what follows. For the purposes of this narrative she will be known (and please forgive the facetiousness) as Anna Mendment.

9.12.90

Dear Mr O'Dale
    I understand that you have enquired as to the whereabouts of Anna Mendment. I think I may be able to help you. Would you be so kind as to explain your interest?
            Yours sincerely,
            Jennifer Crown

Once the little euphoric leap had subsided, I began to feel deeply uneasy about this letter. There was an uncomfortable note of suspicion embedded in its final sentence. Why should I wish to know? Who was I to be asking? What concern was it of mine? The note became, moreover, a symphonic cacophony of doubt when I began to rehearse a possible answer. For what could I sensibly say? I had to acknowledge to myself that my wild fixation, and the passion which had quietly fuelled it for more than three decades of my life, owed its genesis to a meeting of four or five hours at a nondescript party. It could not be believed. I had difficulty believing it myself. I replied tersely that I had known Anna at Oxford, had corresponded briefly and had subsequently lost touch. I wished to renew the friendship.

10.3.90

Dear Mr O'Dale,

Thank you for your letter. Since writing to you I have been worrying rather that I may have raised your hopes too high. I have no address for Anna Mendment. She and I were at Lady Margaret Hall together, but knew one another only casually. I caught sight of her briefly while on a visit to Kansas City some seven or eight years ago. The circumstances were such that it was impossible for me to speak to her.

Perhaps, if you wish to take this matter further, you will contact me by telephone, as I would rather not commit anything to paper . . .

She gave her number. I carried it with me for several days before calling her. I was, you understand, afraid. Not of whatever it was that could not (lower the voice) be committed to paper. That hush-hush business only made me laugh. No, I was afraid, rather, that the moment of decision had arrived. As it had, I knew that I was going to take that route to the wronged girl. Why do we always fear the thing that we desire?

Please don't tell me.

Her vocal style, I discovered, was as guarded as her epistolary. Her strangled diction sounded a reproach that anyone should make her speak at all, and she even struggled to admit who she was. When I announced my own identity she gave a little gasp, followed by an 'Oh!' – of regret, it seemed to me, rather than surprise. I am said to be somewhat diffident myself, and our conversation was certainly no an easy one.

'It was a long time ago,' she faltered.

'You didn't speak to her.'

'No, I didn't actually, you see . . . *see* her. Oh dear. This isn't very clear, is it?'

'Frankly, no.'

'Not physically, that is. It was on television. She was.'

'Performing?'

'No.'

On the page this talk perhaps seems to bowl along, but I can assure you that the silences which thrust themselves between the words were spikily painful.

'The surname was different.'

'Yes.'

'But it was unmistakably our Anna. That brow. That mouth.'

And the star-cluster of freckles inside one thigh?

'It was . . . she.'

There was another intermission. I had a vision of her

padding away to the foyer to buy an ice-cream before the main film came on.

'What was she doing?'

'It was in the news.'

'Yes.'

'A court case. Drugs, I'm afraid.'

'Ah.'

'I really can't remember much more, Mr O'Dale. She was . . . helped through the crowd. By policemen.'

'She was . . . on trial?'

'With others. They gave her name, but I don't remember it.'

'When was this?'

'I've looked in my photograph album. For the holiday, you understand.'

'I understand.'

'It must have been January 1983.'

'I see.'

'Yes, January 1983.'

'I see. That's all?'

'That's all I can tell you, Mr O'Dale. I'm sure I must have wasted your time. I'm very sorry.'

And with that thin apology Jennifer Crown left my life for ever, never knowing what vital part she played in its denouement.

My, that does strike a sombre note, doesn't it! Quite inappropriate. No, let there be no moaning at the bar when I put out to sea, but lavish drinks all round. And no flowers, please. A donation to the English language charity of your choice.

A vital part, yes, for you will surely understand that

dear Ms Crown, in giving me practically nothing, set in train the events which see me here today. Consider my options had she been a more thorough informant. Had she given me an address, might I not have written to Anna in America and received a crushing reply? Had she known the details of Anna's life since 1958 would I not, despairing, have considered the journey futile? Had she been privy to the state of Anna's mind . . . But I do not care to speculate. Enough to record that when the editor of the *Times* wrote to sever my contact I regarded it as confirmation of a decision which, though carefully left unformulated, I had already taken.

El Condor Pasa. The Eagle Has Landed. E. Engelbert Has Stopped By. I refer to the aforementioned owner of this leisure complex, as he is pleased to call it. I once suggested to him that it had the ring of a condition dreamed up by a puritanical psychiatrist. He has the most expressive pair of eyebrows I have ever seen. We spoke just now, to my great surprise, about real estate prices, a subject on which my mind remains a *tabula rasa*, thanks to the use of sophisticated meditative techniques at crucial moments. He raided my biscuit tin, as is his custom, and urged me anew to use the facilities 'while you're still here with us'. This may or may not have been a hint, but I am well aware that whole families of zestful make-believe lumberjacks will soon require my cabin and are prepared to pay good money for their afflictions. Time presses, therefore. Not until this manual is finished shall I succumb to the temptations of the boating lake.

To Whom It May Concern. Mr Thoite's boats are made of seasoned timber and fully comply with all legal requirements. The boats are inspected once every year, according to the regulations. The necessary licenses, certificates of competence etc may be inspected during normal business hours at the offices of THOITE OZARKS REAL ESTATE & DEVELOPMENT INC, CARTHAGE, MISSOURI. There has never been a single accident at Mr Thoite's leisure complex attributable to negligence.

Arranging the end of a life is at once a disturbing and an exciting experience. A way of life, I mean. It had been such a routine existence, and for so long. How terrible to know that it was soon to disappear, and for ever! The dull inevitability of the early morning trudge past flaking Edwardian terraces to buy my morning milk and the newspaper seemed suddenly, now that it was inevitable no longer, a journey tinged with sanctity, some kind of secular pilgrimage. Perched over my poached egg at lunchtime, listening to the daily radio soap opera, I would find myself lamenting that I would never again know this cosy familiarity, this rootedness.

And my flat. Bought with Uncle Mory's legacy, it had never been modernised, and had I been the kind of man who entertains I should have found it unbearably cramped. More, there was a view of a gas-holder from the bedroom, the pub across the road played loud music until late and the neighbours were rough, untidy, unhelpful. It was home to me, however, and the scene of all my private mental and spiritual battles after I left the monastery. It had its invisible marks of holiness. Yet, how strange: I put it on the market and trembled to see the estate agent's man hammering the board into place. (No, no, this was outside Harbin's territory.) I felt ineffably sad and frightened. But when, a few weeks later, someone offered cash, I thought only of my journey, and rejoiced.

Funnily enough, I never once began to imagine the wonderful, dreadful moment of my meeting with Anna until, after the inevitable delay (the unbearable lateness of Boeing), I was on the aeroplane from Heathrow. It was my first flight, and I spent the first part of it as I suppose all tyro aviators do, by turns nervous and stimulated, craning for a view of cloud from a distant window, reading all the small print on the sick bags (by no means big sacks, I registered), struggling to rescue little scraps of food from plastic and cellophane. It was an hour or two before my legs began to ache, but the pain increased very quickly. Striding up and down the aisle gave relief to me, but it obstructed the hostesses with their endless trolleys and infuriated passengers who were trying to watch a film. Manners are not what they were. Forced back to my seat, I was obliged to take up ridiculous postures in order to ease the cramp, so that when my thoughts turned at last to my reunion with Anna they were (to use the word in an appropriate physiological sense) sympathetically strained and agitated. They became waking dreams.

Schema one: she runs down the steps of a large public building, hails a taxi and is about to get in when she spots me approaching. Recognition. I call her name. She smiles, but the smile freezes. She climbs inside the taxi, covers her head with a blanket (where did it come from?) and is whisked away.

Schema two: a long view of a meadow in mist. Two people walk slowly away, arm in arm, talking earnestly. They turn. He remains standing, but she approaches what must be a camera (this is being filmed). When she gets close we see that her face grimaces in anger, and her fist beats against the lens.

Schema three: two lovers in a rowing boat. They glide downstream, a ruddy sun descending into fluffy cloud behind them. His arms are extended round her. They draw closer, her head tilting towards him. As they pass we see that their faces are oval voids of impenetrable blackness.

Schema four: a police court. She stands in the dock, dressed in black, her eyes streaming. The counsel for the defence (ah, it is myself) argues eloquently, violently for her innocence. She throws off a veil and steps forward vindicated, her arms outstretched. But her advocate is snatched away from her and disappears from view. He is the guilty party.

The plane droned on and on; my legs hurts indescribably; my head throbbed. I declined an alcoholic drink and sipped a nasty sweet lemonade. There was no turning back. For good or ill I had sold everything I possessed, and the proceeds were earmarked for my quest, every last penny. It was for ill, my mood informed me. Every last cent. Let it dwindle to nothing. I hated flying.

By the way, if you wish to analyse my transAtlantic dreamlets I am quite content. The merest amateur could do it: tuppeny-coloured dramas reeking with the curdled juices of betrayal and guilt. (Invent your own scoring system.) It is, in any case, far too late for any coyness on my part. But please, please don't imagine that I followed Anna in order to beg and grovel. Certainly not. That, as the poet wrote, is not it at all, not it at all.

You'd like to see me on my knees, imploring forgiveness? Yes, you probably would. The world is crammed full with petty moralists. You'd have me confess myself more vile than the beasts of the field. Forgetting your own human failings, you miserable hypocrite, you'd have me make a cruel mock of myself, the great hairy ape with the distended member!

Let's. Keep. Calm.

This is what I shall say. It was wrong to force, to violate. There are standards of behaviour one should seek to uphold. They are essentially trivial but have their crucial place in a decent, well-ordered society. One should not take another's purse. One should not shout loudly in the streets after midnight. One should obey traffic signals. It is proper that these things should be recognised, and that laws should exist to uphold them. That is all the little I have to contribute on the subject.

We landed. I found a hotel. In the morning your private investigator began to make his travel arrangements. People were polite; telephones worked; timetables were straightforward. The ache in the thighs gradually subsided. Nothing whatsoever went wrong. I am not superstitious about this: presumably things may go wrong all the time or, feasibly, right all the time. What I have learned, however, is never to trust the encouraging sign. This axiom was at that time unknown to me, and I would have laughed indulgently had anyone proposed it. On the last day of February I arrived by Greyhound bus in Kansas City. By the third day of March I had contacted the city's largest newspaper, had been given permission to search the archives and had found, had triumphantly found, the information I had been seeking.

Let us observe the sleuth in his glory. He sits in a low-ceilinged room under flickering fluorescent tubes, a heavy file of newspapers open on the desk before him. If he seems methodical, this is because he is pathologically unable to resist a tempting headline. The hands on that old-fashioned clock on the wall are moving steadily on, with nobody aware of its tedious message but us. We notice a pad and pencil at his side, but he has forgotten what he came for. He yawns contentedly, smooths the page with the rim of his hand. Wake up! we long to shout at him. Look at that picture on your right, columns five, six and seven! And at last he does. he sits upright and his eyes widen. Is that a little chuckle that we hear? He looks about him, wanting to share his jubilation, but the room is empty. Now he leans forward, reads the text very carefully, picks up pad and pencil. Can you make out those letters HB? He begins to scribble . . .

I thought we should savour that exemplary moment. It was, to use the idiom, downhill all the way after that. Consider: I have been in this country rather more than a year; have travelled countless thousands of merciless miles; have spent tens of thousands of dollars, of *pounds*, on transport, food and lodgings, newspaper advertisements, bribes, the hire of private detectives; have suffered irreparable emotional wear and tear; and I know, at the conclusion of all this, nothing of what I wanted to know. Might I express this more simply? Okay, buddy, I'm broke and I'm busted.

It was Anna in the picture, without a doubt. She had been convicted of possessing heroin, but found not guilty of dealing in it. Six months. Strange, but even then the awfulness of it failed to touch me. That came later, when I knew more. Ever since talking to Jennifer Crown I had been aware of at least the accusation of a drugs offence, but my mind somehow avoided any connection between present troubles and the girl I had known. The quest was all, I suppose. Now I made a note of her name (shall we dub her Anna Nimmity in her married guise?) and walked from the newspaper offices with a swagger and a bounce.

Interview A (Date: April 25, 1991. Location: a cold, square, unadorned room in a police station, Kansas City. Interviewee: Mart Loebek, drugs enforcement officer. He is casually dressed, a windcheater and jeans. My ignorance amuses him, provokes him to indiscretions)

– Don't get the idea that this broad was some kind of innocent. She was deep in it. She was lucky not to go down for years.

– I've read the reports.

– Sure, misuse of heroin. Maybe she found a few ounces lying around on her dressing table, eh?

– Isn't that possible?

– Look, I was on that case from the beginning. There was a ring, it was very big money. We got some of those guys put away for the best part of their useful lives. She wasn't blameless young hanger-on. She was none of those things, come to think of it.

– Then why?

– You get the deal you can, Mr O'Dale. We cleaned up pretty well, so good luck to her.

– Can you tell me about her?

– What do I say? An intelligent woman, I guess. She didn't communicate too much, though. She didn't really seem to care. None of those anguished pleadings of innocence you often get. No tears, for sure. She was harder.

– I need to see her. There seem to be no Nimmities in the telephone directory.

– No idea, fella.

– Someone who might know?

– Her old partners, maybe. A few are out.

– Could you suggest?

– Hell, I should get paid for this! Give me that pencil.

Mr Loebek, I should record, is one of those rare informants who did not require any payment for his help. I thank him for that, and for his obliging off-the-record comments.

Now a necessary explanatory note regarding my interviews. Perhaps the consecutive lettering suggests comprehensiveness. Very far from it! I must have spoken to a hundred people on my travels, very few of whom could tell me anything of substance. If this account should by chance appear neat and ordered, allow me to fix an image in your mind – of an increasingly haggard individual dashing this way and that across the vastness which is the United States of America; beating on doors that will not be opened; arriving for appointments which will not be kept; returning to towns whose written and human archives he has already exhausted, lured by fresh hope that remains unfulfilled. That is the investigator's lot, my friend. Knowledge is not quickly won.

Interview B (Date: July 18, 1991. Location: a cafeteria in Brazil, Indiana. Interviewee: Charlotte McNee. She has ordered a double portion of burger with fries)

– We were friends at first school, right, and sort of acquaintances after that, but there was a big gap while she went off to university and did those kinds of things, right, and so we never saw much of each other afterwards. She went to Minnesota as I recall and then to your Oxford in England.

– And she spoke of that?

– Of Oxford, you mean? No, sir, we weren't on those kind of terms, the sort where you swap notes about what you were doing before, right, we simply brushed now and then in our social life. But I have to tell you I saw her going off the rails right early on, and there was no way she wasn't going deeper in trouble when I met up with her again I'm telling you, should we have another coke?

– Off the rails? Anna?

– Well look, mister, I'm not going to sit here and say bad things about an old friend that I have no need of saying, right, but she was always one for doing the dangerous kind of thing. Not physically I don't mean, not parachuting and joy-riding cars, I mean with boys and taking journeys away, skipping school, that kind of thing at an early age, right, there was always that wild streak about her.

– But very bright.

– That's as maybe, and you're absolutely right, I couldn't agree more with you there, she was way ahead of the rest of us and certainly left me trailing, sir, when it came to studies, right, but she was always, I don't know how to say this, loose I suppose you could say. But no I won't, I'll take that back, and say that maybe it was just that she enjoyed a good time, right, and didn't always know when to say no to it.

– Afterwards, you said. Yes, finish them off, I'm not hungry. When she came back.

– Well then, sir, she had her baby, and I did wonder, I mean we all did, who the father might be, which sounds awful, but she was popular, right, and liked the boys, and the first time I saw her with the baby I almost burst out with something like Who gave you that? but luckily held my tongue, have you swallowed something you shouldn't?

– When? Did? She have the baby?

– Straight after she was back, or maybe she brought it back, I wasn't a real friend in those days, right, but yes, as soon as she was back home again and for a real short time before they took it off her or she disposed of it or however you like to look at it, depending what the real truth was. I never knew.

– But the date. Which year was this? Please.

– Oh I'm not the one to ask about dates, mister, can't remember the year I was born unless I think real hard about it, never was one for that history. Has to be about the time I worked in the bakery, I suppose, and yes it was when I had Prince because I remember now, while I was taking care not to ask Who gave you that? he was leaping up alongside her trying to sniff, and the little baby girl, she was bawling her head off, shall we manage a piece of that apple pie?

– Does that help you to pinpoint the date, Charlotte? A slice of pie if you can!

– Help me work this out then. If I was born in . . . 1939, and I was first employed by Mr Jenners, right, he ran the flower shop, I loved the fragrance then, and I must have been sixteen years old, right, working part-time and then full-time, and I suffered four years all that standing on my feet and being paid so bad, I know four years because I started at Eastertime and finished then, too, so I've always remembered. Well then, I went straight in the bakery, and after six months got the room with Mrs Bradley which meant because of the garden I could keep a puppy, and that's just about the time it was.

– When's your birthday, Charlotte?
– January fifteenth. Every year!
– And how old was the baby?
– That first time, sir? Well I don't suppose more than a month or two at most. Very tiny. I never could do such a thing myself, but somehow she let it go, because soon after that she was without it and we never saw it again, ever.

Calm. Keep calm. I calculated as she spoke, and I calculated very carefully afterwards. If you enjoy brain-teasers, as I very much hope you do, perhaps you would like to work it our for yourself. Shall I give the answer on another page, upside down? No, let's clear this up immediately: The child was not mine. Nearly, one might say, but not quite. I really cannot say how I would have reacted if my urgent computations had proved otherwise. Not with sentimental joy, I'm sure. Not necessarily with any kind of pleasure at all. Whatever normal fatherhood must feel like, this could not partake of it. At the time, even knowing it impossible, I imagined a kind of internal adjustment of the compass, a scarcely perceptible turning, like one of those huge oil tankers which swing with slow and stiff laboriousness but nevertheless are at last seen headed in a new direction. Mere asininity on my part.

I arrived at length at tom-tom day. This, at least, has been my pet name for it ever since – if one can make a pet of so loathsome a creature. Ah, I spot a weakness that had never occurred to me before: the smart readers will reasonably imagine that cats are involved. Witty, but wrong. No, the tom-tom expresses the beating of a drum.

The drum is my heart, and the significance of the palpitating doubleness will soon become evident. Coincidental tomatoes also make an appearance, but it's a poor enough fancy, in all conscience. Don't give another thought to it.

Banal settings. I had come to Los Angeles one October dawn, swishing in to the centre on a Greyhound bus while the early sun was still scrapping with yesterday's smog. I lacked proper sleep. That afternoon I was to see a man who had, so fickle rumour proposed, once lived with Anna in New Jersey. I was not swollen with hope. The rooming house I found (for the money had almost gone) was a slum with bare boards and naked light-bulbs. I left my suitcase there and, remembering that this was one of the few places where I had a poste restante arrangement, called in at the office. There were three envelopes waiting for me, and I stuffed them into a pocket.

Banal. In Joe's Diner (yes, I'm sorry) I ordered a tomato juice with ice. I sipped it overlooking a broad boulevard strung with moving cars. Like rosary beads. A man at the next table was coughing moistly. The coffee machine roared and gulped.

The first letter was from the *Times*. Some pedantic underling in the accounts department had been entrusted with a closing down operation on the O'Dale file and had discovered a discrepancy. With the letter came a cheque for £4 12p.

Junk mail is like one of those bugs said to infest computers, contaminating the system for future generations without number. It is, I suspect, immortal. There will be free coupons and obliging offers pursuing each one of us

215

beyond the corners of the globe to the purlieus of eternity itself. Will St Peter hand them over? The second envelope offered life assurance at ridiculously favourable rates: *yes, you, MR D. O'DALE, can take advantage* . . .

I ordered another tomato juice and gave the contents of both envelopes to the waiter for the trash can. (Oh sure, I've picked up some of the lingo and you'd better believe it.) He noticed the cheque and returned it, so I asked his name, wrote it on the back and added my signature. We English know how to tip. 'Jeez,' he said, but whether in thanks or from bewilderment I could not say.

The third and largest envelope, brown, felt-tip writing in block capitals, proved to be of the Russian doll variety. Inside was another one, typed and addressed to my London flat: the sender had obviously received news of my wanderlust at the last moment. I opened it and yet another envelope fell out, this one with the single word *Douglas* written on it. The typed letter was from the family solicitor.

10.6.91

Dear Mr O'Dale.

I very much regret to inform you that your Mother passed away, yesterday evening.

You may know, that She had been suffering an Illness, for some time. She asked that the enclosed Note should be forwarded to you, on her Decease.

Perhaps you will contact me, at your Earliest Convenience, so that the necessary Formalities may be, speedily, dealt with.

Assuring you at all times Etc.

I do sometimes wonder whether solicitors and estate agents exclusively employ naturalised German secretaries with an atavistic devotion to the Upper Case, the pockets of their Gretchen pinafores uncomfortably stuffed with surplus commas.

The tomato juice had the texture of cold porridge. It had become an objective correlative.

My dear son,

I hope that you will be able to shed a tear for me when I have made that journey to the country 'from whose bourn no traveller returns'. We have not been close for many years, and this has been a great sadness to me.

Do you remember, as I so warmly do, the happiness we all shared together when we lived, you and I, with Hettie and Jack? Do you remember that wonderful holiday on the Isle of Wight? We had such fun on the beach, swimming in the warm, clear water. I do hope those memories still mean as much to you as they do to me all this long time after.

The other day I discovered, at the bottom of a drawer, something you have probably forgotten. It was that telescope Uncle Mory bought you one birthday. I really believed that you would become an astrologer one day! It is here for you to collect, with very little else, I'm afraid. I have lived rather hand-to-mouth all my life.

Douglas, please forgive me for not being the best mother there ever was. I was so very proud of you when you went to University. I hope that

217

everything that has happened since has not made you very unhappy, but I fear that it has. I know I have not been good at understanding. Life was difficult for me. I wonder if you understand how much.

Please say a prayer for me. You will know the words to use.

Your loving mother

Interview C. (Date: october 21, 1991. Location: a children's playground in Los Angeles. Interviewee: Robert Shale. He is younger than expected – about 35 – tall, lean, clean-shaven, his hair tied in a pony tail. His manner is guarded and expansive by turns. He has a twitch. He has chosen the meeting place, and during the interview he plays on the swings, slide and other equipment like an overgrown child. There is a roundabout in the guise of a huge red tomato)

– Sure we were together. About '75 that was. We lived like man and wife for a time. Or woman and boy, maybe. Hey! She was my big momma.

– What I wanted to know was.

– Why, man? What's it to you, then? You tell me. I'm a little nervous of you.

– A friend. I'm an old friend.

– Then what's your name. Tell me again.

– Douglas O'Dale.

– No, I never heard her talk of you.

– It was a long time ago.

– Don't know that name. It's a strange name, yeah?

– At Oxford.

– Mississippi?

– No. In England.

– Oh, England! Yeah, she'd been there. She'd been everywhere.

– Did she tell you about it?

– No more than in a casual way I don't suppose.

– People she met, perhaps? Things that . . . happened to her?

– Not so that I recollect it, no. But that's a long time back now. My mind's been ten rounds with Life, man. And I'm talking heavyweight division.

– Did she talk about the past?

– No more than anyone else ever does. But she did talk of it, sure. She'd seen troubles, Anna had. She'd come down a long way. She was bumping along the bottom with me. We had good trips, good times. Hey, come on down this little baby. Waaaagh-eeeeeeeee!

– Troubles?

– Yeah, you know what they are? I know what they are.

– What troubles did she have?

– Personal things, you know. Things maybe she wouldn't want talked about. Why you need to know?

– As a friend.

– A friend. Is that so? Anna always had too many of those. Real good friends. I used to warn her about those guys. What did you ever do for her?

– Me?

– Did you ever sing to her when she was feeling lonely? Did you spend your last dime on dope for her when she was down? I did that. Hey, rock and roll, rock and roll, you been on one of these chickens? Crazy! Were you one of those friends who let her down?

– Did she read a lot?

– Did she *what*?

– Read. She was a scholar. English Literature.

– Is that so?

– Didn't she ever talk about that? Did she say whether she ever had anything published?

– Hey, I think you're kidding me. We're talking about the same Anna Nimmity?

– T.S. Eliot, for instance. Do you remember?

– I think you're a strange guy. Are you strange? Should I be trusting you?

– I thought you might know.

– A weirdo. I've got your number. Hey, climb on this thing.

– I'd rather not, thank you.

– Sure, it's a gas. Hear me, man. I never once saw her touch a book in all the time. You need to lift your legs off the ground, they're too goddam long. She did like movies, though. Hey!

– Drugs.

– How's that?

– I said.

– You're allowed to hold the rail, man.

– She had. A drugs. Problem.

– No problem, man, not when I knew her. Grass, that was all.

– A court. Case. Kansas.

– Sure, that's what her good friends did for her later on. Or so I heard. Woooooo! Got her on the hard stuff. You don't trade in that poison?

– Do I. Seem the. Type?

– She was restless, see? Always. She wanted more than this poor boy could give her.

– And now?

– Now? Hey, you're looking white, man! What does that mean – now?

– I mean. Where. Is she? You. Don't know?

– She ain't nowhere.

– Don't. Understand.

– Nowhere! You really don't know that? The Big C got her years back, poor lady. The mainline variety. He weren't no friend to her neither.

I was, for the record, aggressively sick in a corner of the playground. Yes, it did feel wilful. Rationality cannot be expected of us in such circumstances. My reaction was anger, not sorrow. The tom-toms of the war dance. I wanted to shout loudly in my mother's ear, to wave a fist before Anna's face.

And what might I have said to them, had my wish been granted? I rehearsed a few speeches, I would tell my mother, perhaps, that she had long since been superseded, her totem melted down and re-cast in other forms. How easy to deride her counterfeit maternal pieties! 'As for prayers,' I would add, 'mine are all used up. Invent your own. And do invoke your insipid Romantic poets sparingly. God must get extremely bored with the same old verses.'

Anna would claim my gravest scorn. To have fooled me for so long! The base deception! I would scoff at the wreck of a life, the wastage. 'And is this the superior soul who sneered at Eliot for his timorousness?' I would savagely demand. 'Have you (please forgive the awful poignancy of the question), have you by any faint chance learned to devalue what you have become?'

Calm.

I would ask questions, too. Have you any to propose? Ah, you would have me ask forgiveness! You'll never understand. Very well, I shall imagine myself prostrate. How might she reply?

Take it as read, one version has her shrugging. *After what I've been through, that was nothing. Let's pretend it never happened.*

Or she is found to be consumed by bitterness: *Of all the shits I've come across in my life, O'Dale is at the top of the list. Thieves, murderers, dope-peddlers – they come nowhere near this guy for sheer malodorous viciousness.*

That sounds not a bit like Anna to me. I fear that I have lost the tone of her voice. It fades to the thinness of a ghost.

Incident? What incident? I also hear. *I don't have the slightest memory of what you're wailing about.*

I wonder if you realise which of these replies would be the most terrible to me.

And if she indeed remembered, if she recalled every sensation with a vividness of colour and sound and smell and feeling, how would she describe what happened that night? If I should, nervously, ask 'How was it for you?' would she spit or sigh or weep? Might she, just possibly, speak of pleasure? Or might her face split into a grin?

T*he sight of you that night* she burbles cruelly *with those comical trousers hoist inches above your feet, like some spindly circus clown! I had a job not to roll around on the grass laughing, believe me. Your hair plastered down after that tumble in the pool, your face white as a sheet, your filthy teeth like weed-covered rocks on some polluted foreshore! Oh, that tedious conversation, you forcing me to talk about the superlatively boring T.S Eliot who I'd had enough of to last me a lifetime and had already vowed never to read again, and then the vapid childhood reminscences I had to dredge up simply in order to break the awful black silences! Finally, of course, that rigmarole in the car, me unable to believe for a moment that such a spectacle as you could have any but the most prosaic intentions, learning my error too late, and that hilarious conclusion, typical O'Dale farce, when at the crucial moment, the ecstatic, swimming moment, the goddam dog. . .*

I do not wish to hear this. Am I smiling? That part of the brain which stimulates laughter begins to vibrate, but nothing at all comes of it.

. . . goddam Dalton Wymberly's goddam faithful Airedale finds a tempting pair of buttocks perched on proud display in the family car and sinks its teeth deep into tender flesh!

Calm. I loathe dogs. Let's keep calm.

I felt, I say, anger rather than sorrow. I felt, too, as if I were shipwrecked, marooned in some arid landscape between my old life and what I had been seeking. I could hear the waters lapping. The days passed by, but one was the same as another. I had, at that time, only one further meeting arranged, and I resolved to honour it merely because that it what one does. There was no means of escape, and no direction to aim for even had a ship appeared on the horizon.

Interview D (Date November 1, 1991. Location: a wooden shack within sight and sound of the sea at Carmel, California. Interviewee: Suzie Kepler. She is a soft-spoken woman in her late forties. Her interiors are hung with rugs, the floor littered with colourful cushions. She wears beads and has moccasins on her feet.)

– When I was young I was a little foolish, and Anna Mendment was the kindest person to me there ever was. That was when I lived in a commune just outside San Francisco. I was only in my teens, I'd run away from home, and she seemed much older and wiser. I suppose she was only about twenty-three herself then.

– What kind of person was she. Literary, yes?

– She'd read her books, certainly. She knew a thousand quotations, and not only from Kerouac and Ginsberg, as the rest of us did. This was early Sixties, remember. And she'd pick up a book now and then.

– Only now and then?

– When the mood was on her. You have to know that Anna was a trouble person, Mr O'Dale. Again, that's something I see more clearly now. We all believed we were in some kind of a heaven then, for a while at least. I think even Anna believed that some of the time. It was a holy place, with peace, good vibes, sharing. But perhaps Anna could see much more clearly what it was she was escaping.

– Escaping?

– The world she left behind. She would tell me about it, you see. She confided in me. I was pupil and confessor. That's hindsight again. We'd sit side by side on our prayer mats, maybe on the verandah looking out over the hills, smoking hash. It was incredibly beautiful. Would you care for a joint?

– No. Thank you.

– Then she'd tell me. Sometimes about her child-hood. Sometimes about the people she'd known most recently. Mostly, though, random thoughts which picked up these things on the way and dropped them off in just the same offhand fashion. That's when some of her book-learning came out – theories, poems, even chunks of prose.

– Strongly argued, yes? Coherent. Forceful.

– That's not how it was then. I don't know whether you remember right, Mr O'Dale, or whether she changed. What I recall is that she would slide from one thought to another without hard logic. That may have been the pot talking We didn't have much reverence for logic. Still don't, speaking for myself.

225

– Did she mention, for instance, her time in England?

– Oh yes, sure. She was up at Oxford, wasn't she? She liked that, I think. She did tell me things.

– What things?

– The look of the place, as I recall. The fine old buildings. Taking boats out on the river. She showed me a picture of that. With poles, was it?

– Punting.

– Right! I remember, see?

– Did she talk about parties?

– I guess so. That kind of thing.

– But any in particular? A party outdoors, perhaps, at a country house?

– Not that I recall, Mr O'Dale. This is history, you know. But she had good times there for sure. I don't recall a single bad thing she said about your country.

– Or the people? Did anything horrible happen to her in England?

– I really think not. No, the bad things started as soon as she got back here. The trouble with her family and all.

– What was that about?

– That was about the baby. By the time I knew her the baby had gone. That was part of her trouble, I guess. She couldn't forgive them. Said they'd betrayed her. She and Joe thought they'd keep it, but that didn't work out. It wasn't allowed to happen.

– Joe?

– Nimmity. He was a big, lively man. The cops got

him on some kind of robbery charge and so I never knew him really well. But he had charisma.

– He was the father?

– Sure. This is how Anna told it. She said she met Joe on the flight back from England and they declared ardent love with their eyes all the way across the Atlantic. Not a word said. It was the overwhelming clutch of the heart for them both. You believe in that kind of thing? Very Sixties, maybe, but I still do. Anyhow, he was already living the commune, he was the leading light, and they had the baby there. I mean, the birth was on a rug in the main room with everybody gathered round chanting. It must have been such a beautiful experience. But there'd been some trouble with the police already, and the social people were pushing in, and then her parents got the baby taken away. Said she wasn't a fit mother, that kind of thing. Other people told me Anna was never the same after that. She had the black moods that I'd sometimes see, though she was pretty good at covering them. She'd suddenly switch from despair to this incredible brightness. I thought she was such a wonderful person.

– She never saw the baby again?

– She wasn't even supposed to know where it had gone They'd changed the little girl's name, everything. Put her to foster parents. I don't know the details, but it was that kind of deal. Anna was tenacious, though. She told me she knew all bout her. I do believe she sent presents from time to time.

Then the commune began to break up, and Joe came out of prison and they disappeared out east somewhere. When I next saw her, five or six years later, she and Joe had split, she didn't have that brightness any more and she didn't mention the baby once.

– Would you know how to find her?

– Lord, she's dead!

– No, not Anna. The baby. The daughter.

– Find the daughter? I sure as hell couldn't take you to her, but I do have an idea how you'd find out. But why on earth would you want to do a thing like that, Mr O'Dale?

I forget what answer I gave her. Probably it sounded sensible: why shouldn't a man look up the daughter of an old friend, even in these unusual circumstances? Perhaps I invented some keepsake which I felt she ought to have. Yes, I believe I burbled on about a brooch. (I do, after all, have a capacity for lying, if only about trivial things.) The inevitability of the quest so seized me that, scribbling down the names and addresses she gave me, I felt no need of designing an answer for myself. I left that shack in a spirit of befuddled determination.

There is no sensible answer. For months I have doggedly foot-slogged the dull townships of these sprawling Ozark Mountains, prying and snooping, ferreting, gawping, yet I am still unable to say to what purpose. Even now that I can proudly claim 'mission accomplished', I find a satisfactory explanation impossible. What did I think to achieve? What kind of resolution could there possibly have been? I had no notion, should such a lurid thought have crossed your mind, that I might discover an Anna clone through whom I would achieve grace and atonement by re-staging, less violently, that earlier act: I hope you feel thoroughly ashamed of yourself for having such an idea. I must have known, surely, that there was nothing healing she could say. I knew better than to hope for evidence of some lingering remembrance of me.

I arrived in cold December, with three hundred dollars in my wallet and enough small change for a few telephone calls. The imminence of penury did not depress me in the slightest. Searching for Anna had always been frustrating, but now I sensed that I was closing in on my prey. The early calls were successful. Unguarded tongues wagged gabbily. How delicious the snug knowingness of the homing sleuth! How cosily gratifying his one-way intimacies! I would find myself assuming voices, enjoying husky exchanges with characters whose precise role in the plot they themselves could not possibly understand. Why, many of them were ignorant of the plot itself!

With almost indecent haste I discovered her name; where she lived; the business of her employer. Too soon: I should have felt a gauche interloper indeed had I confronted her in the raw nakedness of those incomplete investigations. No, I needed to steal up on her through the tangled undergrowth of her circumstances, through the murmuring thickets of her acquaintances. Let her at last emerge from this camouflage already known! I kept my distance, fled any threat of a sighting. Guileless tongues sang garrulously. Seemingly innocent questions elicited more and more information for my swelling dossiers: the name of her hairdresser, something she once said to a taxi driver, the newspaper she read. These were her ways. I carried a small notebook and jotted down street names, advertising slogans, the destinations on the boards of buses, snatches of overheard conversation. This was her world. Oh yes, it was quite unnecessary, most of it, a self-indulgent madness. How I relished it! I saw myself approaching her with sly expertise, taking my time, sussing her out, as they say. I was your archetypal American private eye. I knew the score, and I drew ever closer.

And with what feverishness I crept forward those last remaining yards! It was a morning in early January, flecks of rain tossed from a grey-bellied sky. The epiphany could be put off no longer. All my information was in place. alighting from the bus, I knew precisely where she would be in ten minutes' time, how she would arrive, what she was doing there. Gusts of wind wafted air rich in negative ions, but I could scarcely breathe. Out of the bus station, along a narrow street with a garage at one end, across a car park: there was a detailed map inside my head. I skirted a shopping mall. It was a dream landscape. I knew my way, although I had never been there before. The doctor's surgery was beyond a patch of grass, a simple brick building stand on its own . . .

Calm. Calm. Calm.

I face a difficulty, and crave an indulgence. Anna's daughter is largely ignorant of her past: she knows nothing more than that she was adopted as a young child, and she remembers nothing of consequence. She is, for reasons which I cannot in the circumstances explain, very likely to forage through this manuscript. Who am I to reveal her true parentage? I trust the reader will forgive, therefore, a few tinkerings with the literal truth. A colour, a manufacturer's label, even a phrase, will occasionally be tampered with in the interests of protecting that innocence. I accept the charge that even to advertise my intentions may alert her to the truth. All I can reply is that she has not, in my humble opinion the staying power to persevere with long words in long paragraphs, any more than she has sufficient intellect to tease out meanings from verbal circumlocutions. I mean, I suppose, that she is incapable of understanding any but the most obvious of clues – and if I defame you, madam, please forgive me. I never was a good judge of character.

There was no shelter outside the surgery. I had to stamp my feet to keep warm. Her car was already parked outside: a blue Vauxhall convertible, 1987 model; road tested three weeks earlier; garage bill $140.57, including some work on the exhaust system. If the appointments were running to schedule she would be in with the doctor by now: Vanessa Lightblum, who had treated her for the last eleven years. The current problem was a sore ankle. She had been limping for two weeks and a day. I circumnavigated the building several times, nervous, fearful, terrified. The rain began to thicken.

She came out. I knew what to expect and I didn't know. Thirty-two years old. Five feet five inches. Mesomorph, bolstered by cellulite: there is a density that shapes her end. Auburn hair. Grey-blue eyes. A very small scar above the right eyebrow from a childhood cycling accident. She wore a pale raincoat. Sensible brown shoes with low heels. Benfields Department Store, first floor, Winter Sale Now On. How do the police ever catch criminals using details of that sort? They miss the essential, throbbing part of a human being. She was all of those things and yet quite separate from them . . . herself.

I ran away. No, I walked in the other direction with my usual poise, but I was certainly escaping. I wished, you see, to experience nothing more than a fleeting glimpse at that stage. It seemed somehow proper, decorous. It would be gross to make a great drama of that very first sighting. After all, my opinion of her might be eternally coloured by chance circumstances: the weather, my mood, her limp. A gradual accretion of impressions was called for, a concatenation of performances in which, however oblivious of it she was herself, she was cast in the leading role. I resolved to wait and watch.

Come with me on a tour of the area. We are not, I'm afraid, taking the scenic route. The countryside is varied here (streams, wooded valleys, high ridges), but she is, with one rather artificial exception, a creature of the urban landscape. Here is a typical shopping scene, at a hyper-market on the edge of town: we are tracking a youngish woman who pushes a trolley loaded with the usual mixture of colourful convenience foods and low-fat conscience-soothers. Ah, it is she! The limp is scarcely noticeable now, thank goodness. We have to squeeze through a gap between her trolley and the shelf with the lavatory cleaning materials. She gives a weak smile which does not disguise the irritation at the mouth corners, and then she is gone. Or we are gone . . . Now admire the prodigious display at a downtown sandwich bar, with more choice than is decent: the Americans do these things so much better than us. She is before us in the throng, but the hard-pressed counter assistant doesn't see her. What embarrassment! He asks *us* for our order, and we indicate her priority with an expressive inclination of the head. She nods in return, acknowledgement rather than gratitude, her head full of double pastrami-on-rye and suchlike. (She is buying for her boss who, as I have come to know, has a healthy appetite.) . . . On to the public library, where she always makes for the fiction section. Something light and unsteamily romantic. It's always surprising, and a little amusing, to take a book from a shelf and come face to face with another browser similarly engaged! She drops hers, and we smartly nip round the corner and retrieve it for her: *Cicely Crupt's Crafty Concealments*. No, no, but something in a similar vein. Did that muttering perhaps contain a word of thanks?

We spoke at last. I mean we met, to all outward show as any new acquaintances meet, not as hunter and hunted. I joined the camera club, parting with a precious ten dollars for the privilege. Her colour prints of mares and foals won third prize in the 'Cuddly Creatures' category, and I admired them, lavishly.

'Haven't I seen you somewhere before?' she asked.

She is not, as you will have realised, observant. We chatted idly. The English are still, for no reason I can readily understand, well regarded by Americans. I was invited to meet Slim, her husband. (Don't be nervous: this is another pseudonym.) We got on well, and I was paraded before their friends as a kind of prize animal. Very soon afterwards she did me a great service regarding my accommodation: I am grateful for this, but am conscious of being on proud display as Tame Englishman Writing Book. It seems that I am a buddy, a good ole boy. 'Stop by whenever you can make it.' I find it hard to credit the brilliance of my achievement.

And to what end?

Let's please keep calm.

But to what end? What did I want from her? If she had been beautiful, perhaps, or blessed with great intelligence . . . . No, that isn't it.

I do realise that I have failed to bring her to life for you. Should I tell you that she and Slim live in a neat little house with its own small yard; that they have been thinking about having children for some time and fully appreciate that they will have to make a decision soon; that they have two cats named Eleanor and Theodore; that she works in an office in Carthage, although her job involves some travel around the area; that Slim has a white-collar job in the local environmental health department; and that they both love country music? Only, I suppose, in order to avoid the unpalatable truth, which is that I heartily, vehemently, dislike the woman.

This is most unfair, but I have a commitment to the truth. As those first sketchy impressions were overlaid by the bolder strokes and hatchings of experience, I came to see that she was narrow-minded, ungenerous, opinionated, self-centred, windy and dull. I have no doubt that she would be upset to hear this verdict, since she seems to worship the ground I walk upon, but I am dangerously emboldened by the fact that we shall never meet again. I am also determined, for once, to have the last word.

Calm.

She called in to see me yesterday, here in my rustic cabin, and asked how the manual was progressing. Time presses, as well she knows. During her first visit, weeks ago, I was still struggling with the opening pages, and I remember being irritated by the gushing interruption.

'How wonderful! This is so clever! What are you going to call it?'

'I suppose something like *O'Dale's Guide to Crossword Puzzle Solving*.'

'Oh, no!' she cried dismissively. 'That's much too plain. We'll think of something neater than that. You want a sexy title!'

Foolish woman. I have decided, in the event, to follow my own less excitable instincts. The title stands.

(As for her suggestion that I provide the reader with blank pages at the end of the book – as 'scribbling sheets' was it, dear God?! – I am afraid that I had to suppress her ravings with such forcefulness that I doubt she will allow the thought to surface in her feeble mind ever again.)

She was not alone in her febrile enthusiasm. As my project took shape, everybody in the neighbourhood offered to help. Even those who had never attempted to solve a puzzle in their lives thought they would dash off a few swift clues according to O'Dale principles. What childish rubbish I tossed into the bin! Her efforts were no exception. I honestly believe the word 'anagram' was new to her at the outset. She sat here for hours, in that battered armchair facing the television set, transposing letters, hunting laboriously through the dictionary for simple words she simply did not know. Torture.

Yesterday I acknowledged to myself that the quest was over. We talked; she left; I knew that it was finished.

Let's keep calm.

It was a day like today. By mid-morning the sun was quite warm, and she suggested that we walk among the trees around the lake. She is a woman difficult to deny.

'You're too white, Douglas. Let's get you some fresh air.'

'But the manual.'

'Almost finished, you told me so. Thought of a title yet?'

It was not her fault. I had to tell myself this repeatedly in order to quell the rage that propelled me through the birches and the pines. She scampered to keep up with me. She prattled brightly about this, that and absolutely nothing, while I tried not to blame her for something she could not in any way help.

'You'll return to England when the book's finished?'

'No, I'll never go back.'

It was not her fault. It was Anna's fault for dying. It was my fault for not striking a bargain with Anna's ghost.

'You're not going home?'

I said something about bad memories, and she shrugged: 'Oh, I don't believe in worrying about the past. It's gone and done with, isn't it?'

But no, I wanted to cry out, *it's not the redundancy of the past, but the banality of the present, that's the horror of it can't you see? For the present to have no resonance, for it to die to nothing like a flat and colourless voice in a room without depth or echo*

What we spoke about, I don't know. About the past,

yes, but I have the scantiest recollection of the conversation. I said very little, I believe. Now and then a phrase of hers would stand clear of the surrounding babble.

'I was abandoned as a baby,' she said, 'but I never give a thought to it. What's the point?'

For the present to be this woman in her dullness, not Anna. For the past to be something she has sprung away from. That's the horror. She and I not between us able to install Anna into the present because she, her daughter, rejects the idea of her, not in bitterness, which would be vital and re-claiming despite itself, but from a sense of futility

Did I begin to talk about a night in England more than thirty years before? I think I must have done, because she put a hand on my arm and spoke consolingly, assuring me that I had nothing to worry about.

'Some people have these terrible guilt feelings,' she said. 'But I don't believe in the past.'

No, no, not guilt. That is not it. Not it at all

'We've all done things we shouldn't.'

Not those time-borne contiguities, not flesh upon flesh. Those, yes, mere bagatelles, those unworthy of our perfervid moralities, but yet flesh on flesh not mere triviality, not merely that

'But what we do is important, after all.'

'Is it? Years afterwards?'

Yes, if those actions part of the eternal, if in those moments we find our grasp commensurate, yes, yes, yes

'The mind's a great healer,' she said.

Then I truly wanted to stifle her, to choke the ignorant cliches in her throat.

'You mean it closes over,' I said. 'It wears a shameful cicatrix.'

'Is that one of your anagrams?' she asked.

'It simply forgets.'

'Thank God, I say.'

Who never wrestled with the shadow of God

'There's plenty of things I'm grateful to forget.'

And then I began to tell her, secretly of course, my mind offering the story to her should she wish to accept it *This is how it was with your mother* and she continued to prate, and the sun continued to beam through the branches, and we continued walking until the path brought us back to the cabin.

Not lust I said *don't think it was lust, never lust as the mainspring, nor love even, not if love mutable, trivial, time-borne, I shan't pretend love, no, but something I sought far profounder, that words only reach at, what seemed, at the awful surrendering moment, graspable* Calm Calm *seemed graspable but was not, for in that sinking moment* Let's please keep calm *in that moment, time of swooning closeness, intermingling, warmth, dark odour, breathing, rhythm, in that deepening moment surged the urgent vicious lust, at last the damnable turbid lust, shrieking Self, demanding penis-pleasure, denying spirit, swamping spirit in sensual clamour, betraying fouling, killing, until at last, betraying, fouling, I took my pleasure, selfish pleasure, mere flesh pleasure, and came to realise my loss*

20 Wary of the Almighty when mad dog fastens upon rear (3-3)

Yes, that was the ultimate in divine pranks, wasn't it, the frisky hound of heaven? The bum's rush for my smart-arse presumption. My *anus miserabilis*. Tarquin very much. Fangs a million, or so it felt. A stern rebuke. Logical, too: Doug/lass/Airedale! I did laugh at that, if not immediately.

It was, we are all agreed, immensely funny.

Have you solved the clue yet? *God-shy.* I invented it myself, and I'm rather proud of it. Don't imagine that it sprang from desperation: there were other possibilities. 'Top spy' would have fitted. I count myself one now, after all.

And the horsy fraternity really needn't bother to tell me that 'rear' and 'shy' are not strictly synonymous. It's too late in the day. I'm tired.

I'm tired of searching for God, whatever it may be.

This is what I like about my little neologism, its proliferation of meanings. Try it for yourself: two points for each one you can think of in five minutes. Are we to assume bashfulness in the presence of the supreme being? Good, good, a tick against that one: you're off the mark!

I did feel that proper diffidence once. For a long time, in fact. How else begin such a search but on your knees? I pleaded, I wept, I fasted in the traditional manner. The piety was positively medieval. I spoke the words. I beat my breast. My knees were raw.

Daft bleeder.

But no, I don't blame myself for that. A sensible patient begins by following the doctor's prescription. (The illustrious Dr Thom-Thom Aquinas, in this case: a rather chilling bedside manner, a stubborn affection for purges and cold-water cures, but his battered old hold-all simply bursts with high-sounding nostrums.) I followed respected professional advice. I kept my surgery appointments. I took my medicine and never once asked for a sugar lump.

But if the treatment doesn't work? If, indeed, you feel worse after that appallingly rigorous treatment than you did before it began? Away with the medical analogy: if, I ask you, this thing you seek will not, *will* not, show itself, then what do you do? You can't guess? Why, roll up, roll up for the God-shy! Every one's a winner!

Actually, I'm afraid, far from it. You know how those coconuts are always set so deep in their rings that it's impossible to dislodge them? That's just how it will be, and with you throwing blindfold to boot. You'll be a laughing stock, but the exercise will do you good. Go on, let off some steam!

I hurled everything I had at the Godhead.

Eventually, wearied beyond weariness, you suspect that there may be nothing there at all. Despair! When you allowed it to have been in hiding you had, at least, your frustration, your anger. But absence? Our world becomes a desert. (I'm about to claim six points.) Your doughty gardener curses a barren soil that's shy of worms, that lacks their busy catalytic digestive processing. It's rather like that, maybe: the universe is simply God-shy, not loamed by a divinity. It has no texture. Its vital compounds lie inert, unprocessed, unusable. It's infertile.

Let's grant the possibility, and shudder.

What would it be like, this universe? It would contain a hundred thousand scattered bones. The void would sound with a solitary laugh that had no meaning. A single shadow would pass across its blackness.

I shudder, don't you?

Ah, but then there's the allure of the final gamble. The last shot. The experiment. The trial. The *shy*.

Eight points to O'Dale!

Here's a question: if there should be a God (I insist that you grant this possibility, too) what might we expect of it? Oh, forget the trite Sunday School lessons. Put down your sacred texts. Don't give me truth, justice, all the rest of those tinny time-borne slogans. They suit us well enough when circumstances permit, but let's not inflict them on the Godhead. Which may, after all, be amoral. Love, you say? But it may have no heart. Wisdom? It may have no mind.

I shall tell you what I think, and then you can laugh. I shan't hear you.

I believe in God the great compiler. (Please dismiss that bearded old chap with his thesaurus: this is unbecomingly childish of you.) I believe in the God of cryptic clues, of subtle allusions, of cosmic anagrams, of teeming cross-references.

I believe in the God of completion.

22 *I'm at first accusative, then cry wildly – at last find grace (5)*

For all things that we know have confluence. For everything we see proclaims a oneness. And yet, how secretly: those southering birds obey the season's hidden promptings; those passing clouds are sweepings from the spume of far-off seas; the earth we tread is weathering of a mountain; a mysterious sympathetic force tethers the inconstant moon.

Is it, then, crass to wish ourselves encompassed?

That's what I shall bawl into the eternal ear at the first opportunity. (I persist, you see.) Is that, I shall demand, an unreasonable desire?

'Dear God of puzzles,' hear me pray. 'Let us be a part of Thy eternal crossword, the smallest syllable in Thy most obscure subterranean clue.'

I should have been a clergyman!

Assuming that I have the courage, I shall next attempt a mild criticism. Why, I shall snarl (should snarling be an option), why give us this modest compiling gift of our own if not to mock us for our inadequacies? That's the only credible inference one can draw, after all, the operation of a divine cruelty.

Don't misunderstand me. (He, of course, won't: such is the nature of things.) I'm not so foolish as to request omniscience. One may only faintly imagine, with trembling, the mighty reach and grasp of the compiler God's most straightforward clue. I'd happily settle for the *Times* myself: it's best to know one's range.

'We feel, oh Lord,' I shall intone, speaking courageously for all Mankind, 'like those exploratory scribbles untidy solvers make in newspaper margins adjacent the holy black-and-white grid: broken parts of words, initials, jumbled letters towards some possible anagram that never works. Our fate is to be crossed through, abandoned.'

Then, whether I am answered or not, I shall adduce some personal evidence: a laugh, a pool, a garden . . .

Shall we imagine that there is a reply. (I have resisted anthropomorphism pretty well so far, don't you think?) Perhaps I am asked to be more specific. *Come, what exactly is it that you crave?* In a booming voice, presumably.

Clever! He knows that our words don't quite fit it! There's no point in consulting a dictionary. What shall I say?

I shall give examples. I shall say:

– willow trees hung over a stream, the lowest leaves tugged by the water, the water whorled and bubbling in its leaf-troubled current

– shadows on a mountain slope, sun and loud and scree in perpetual dance

– a thunder storm at night, the searing jagged lightning flash illuming churning cloud, a forest's bulk, a tossing meadow lashed by rain

Is this yet any clearer? I speak of confluence. I mean to say that the cloud rising out of the ocean, passing over the mountain, masking the tethered moon, drops its rain on the forest, on the meadow, on the soft earth that once was a mountain, in the stream running seawards, where the water is troubled by a willow, in which sits a bird . . .

This is no clearer. I shall further say:

– see the cat in its stalking, cunning, yet oblivious
– see the horse in its running, swift, oblivious
– see the bull in its bellowing, oblivious
– see the mad dog in its biting, oblivious

And I shall cry loud and vicious abuse at the knowledge which separates, which refuses oneness, which denies us brotherhood with the stream and tree and mountain, with bird and beast, with (may God be forgiven!) our fellow man.

For I shall ask:

– does the eagle in its soaring feel separate?
– does the lion in its bloody hunting feel separate?
– does the stag in its rutting feel separate?

These, you understand, will be rhetorical questions. In the silence that follows I shall no doubt (if I survive my blasphemy) reflect upon the many circumstances of my life. I would not wish it to be thought that I have known no happiness. On the contrary, my lot has been an easy one. My health has been good. My pleasures, if commonplace, have been real. Alas, our moments of joy, precisely for being momentary, time-borne, are (or so it seems to me) the very cause of our malaise.

Pleasures to be recorded: the sensuousness of words, the smell of old books, the taste of strong tea, the smile of a close acquaintance . . . No, I have no time for this. There have been many pleasures.

My genial host has just waved a last farewell. He is, I imagine, on his way home to a quarterpounder with fries. Than you, Mr Thoite, for your generosity. The view from my window has been another of my pleasures, the range of low hills, this deep lake with its single boat bobbing.

After that dread silence, if invited to say more, I shall

plead that I dared; that a man who had no natural aptitude for the task did toil and sweat to lose himself in the eternal confluence – and proved, by the attempt, that it could not be done. Shall I be believed?

Ah, but perhaps, after all, I shan't need to be believed! May this final shy of mine, this last shot, not absolve me entirely, not free me from my poor schismatic self?

> *Here lies O'Dale,*
> *Whose wits did not fail,*
> *But, resolved to construe*
> *The ultimate clue,*
> *Sought truth instantaneous*
> *In depths subterraneous;*
> *His final solution*
> *Full-fathomed ablution.*

You like it? Deeply carved, please, on a tombstone of black and white chequered marble. And we really ought to have a motto at the bottom, a finishing flourish which speaks optimistically of the deceased's present condition. *Uproarious treats (2,4)* would be rather good: that's 'At Rest', of course. Or *New self to leap elemental bounds altogether (4,6)*: 'Fell Asleep'. Or perhaps, should there be sufficient space, *Regenerate gent free, no doubt, to roam around new abode (3,4,3,4,6)*. I leave you this cumbersome clue as my last bequest.

Don't be disturbed. Forgive my awful cackling mirth. This febrility is only to be expected. However long one may have considered these matters, prepared oneself, when the moment at last arrives . . .

Hurry up please its time

All things that we know have confluence, proclaim their oneness: the birds, clouds and their skimming shadows, the earth we tread, the trees stooped to the river, the cat in its stalking, Douglas O'Dale in his apparent, his awkward, his comical singularity. Let me believe this.

Let me believe in abstruse interweavings, that they come to have meaning; that mere fragments and phrases may shape into meaning; that stuck phonemes of feeling may form to a meaning; that the shards of our lives may show forth as rich patterns which are more than mere fragments, are subsumed in that meaning.

Let me believe that this dense interfusing consumes all we have thought and seen, all we have felt and uttered; that it takes our joys and our pains; takes our laborious learning; takes our trivial pastimes; takes a girl by a pool and her fugitive shadow; takes the love of a mother, though brittle, uncertain; takes a night in a garden.

Let me believe that there are no voids between us. Let me believe that the black and echoing emptiness we inhabit is a horror which our feeble minds invent; that the chilling laugh we hear rings only round the chambers of our own deceiving brains.

Let me believe that, like the bird in its feeding and the horse in its running, we may know and yet not know.

And let me believe that, in the moment of daring, I shall float without struggle; shall be lapped and enfolded; shall sink into meaning until, surrendering, foundering, I lodge in deep caverns, soft caverns, green caverns, beneath the tug of the waves where the tides do not reach.

Scribbling sheet

Scribbling sheet

Scribbling sheet

Scribbling sheet

Scribbling sheet